The Constellations

The Constellations

Kevin Cunningham

SWITCHGRASS BOOKS   NORTHERN ILLINOIS UNIVERSITY PRESS   DeKalb

© 2012 by Switchgrass Books, an imprint of
Northern Illinois University Press
Published by the Northern Illinois University Press,
DeKalb, Illinois   60115
Manufactured in the United States using acid-free paper.
All Rights Reserved
Design by Shaun Allshouse

Library of Congress Cataloging in Publication Data
Cunningham, Kevin, 1966–
   The constellations / Kevin Cunningham.
      p. cm.
   ISBN 978-0-87580-683-9 (pbk. : acid free paper) — ISBN 978-1-
60909-068-5 (electronic)
   1. Fathers and sons—Fiction. 2. Loss (Psychology)—Fiction. I.
Title.
   PS3603.U666C66 2012
   813'.6—dc23
                           2012030590

To Elizabeth Hart

Acknowledgments

Some writers are sufficiently antisocial to publish a book alone. I am not one of them. My gratitude and thanks to the following: Stuart Rathje and Linda Packer; Russell Primm; Claude Waterman, Michael Kulycky, Judi Mack, Jo Thomas, and Rocco Fumento; Laurie Bernstein; Anthony Labriola; my wife and daughter; and Mark Heineke, J. Alex Schwartz, and the entire staff at Switchgrass Books/Northern Illinois University Press.

The Constellations

THE PHONE RANG AT 6 A.M. It was Dombey, as always as loud as a man who was hard of hearing.

"Roy boy," he exclaimed. "They take the cast off?"

"Yesterday," Roy said.

"How you getting by otherwise?"

"The usual."

"Me and my brother-in-law picked up some more extra work," Dombey said. "If you're up for it with your leg."

"This the brother-in-law who does drywalling?" Roy asked.

"Sometimes. Let's talk about it face-to-face, though."

"My car's iffy."

"I'll pick you up," Dombey said.

Extra work, Roy thought as he hung up. A man never needed it more. He lit a cigarette, already his fourth of the day. Across the table Cammy removed the empty bag from the Cheerios and put the box on her head. Soon the waxy cereal bag was drifting around the room, blown by the kitchen's competing drafts. Grub pounded on the table with a spoon. Upstairs, his son got ready for school.

Eric picked up his last empty and tore off the label. Tin cans worked best for constellations because of their flat bottoms. Aluminum beer cans were more abundant and easier to get a nail through, but the concave bottoms distorted the shapes. Aunt Phyl had declared them off-limits for other reasons, in particular because they made his bedroom smell like a tavern. He didn't mind the odor.

He aimed his flashlight through Boötes, the Herdsman. It threw freckles of light onto the wall. He still needed to wiggle a nail in the hole representing Arcturus, to make it as big as a first-magnitude star deserved.

Aunt Phyl turned on the lamp and flipped off the radio before stooping to root through the cans. She squinted at him. "Did you find that shirt under an old rock?"

"I put my school clothes on last night. So I could sleep longer." Eric thrust out one leg. "My pants, too."

"Your aunt Deborah's going to be here when you get home from school," Phyllis said. "Do you want her thinking you were out all night? And did you sleep with the radio on?"

When Eric arrived in the kitchen his father was sipping his coffee. Eric knelt to pet a cocker-something mix drowsy from a meal of dog food and breakfast cereal. He wore burrs he had picked up a few days before.

"I'm the queen," Cammy exclaimed from under the box.

"You'd certainly think so in this house," Aunt Phyl said.

Roy ran tap water onto the end of his cigarette. The sharp smell of the sulfur in the water mingled with that of the coffee and curled Eric's nose; he had yet to get used to the odor of well water, his father's predictions to the contrary.

"Aunt Deb's coming tonight," Roy said. "To help Aunt Phyl for a little while, now that I'm going back to work. So I want everyone to pick up the house when you get home."

Both older children answered with polite murmurs. In Eric's opinion the house was passably clean. The toilet water was blue. Aunt Phyl had knocked down all the cobwebs. The mice mostly stayed outside now that winter had passed. Before Roy could go on, Buck leapt onto the table and gave a great yawn. He was a weathered old tomcat, left behind by a past occupant of the house and gone half-wild. With a glance he frightened Dusty the house cat back to a hiding place behind the refrigerator.

"He's probably brought in another mouse," Roy said.

"I'll find it," Aunt Phyl said, but she first scooped up Buck and flung him out the door.

"Why can't he stay?" Cammy asked.

"Because he's crawling with disease. It's a wonder we're not all foaming at the mouth." Aunt Phyl began her search for the mouse in the dining room, occasionally calling for the kids to hurry up and eat.

Cammy asked in a low voice, "What if she doesn't find the mouse?"

"We'll smell it eventually," Roy said.

When Roy went to the bathroom Eric eased over to his place, looked into his father's coffee mug to see what remained. Just a few grounds swimming in the brown soup at the bottom, forming and reforming into shapes, now Cepheus, now Libra.

ERIC AND CAMMY LISTENED hopefully to the *whir-whir* from the car, less concerned with the walk to the road than with the color rising in their father's face. "Piece of shit," he finally said and he slammed his hands against the steering wheel. For a moment he stared straight ahead, and Eric watched the red fall down the back of his father's neck and into his shirt, like a thermometer during the passage of a cold front.

"Well, we're going to have to walk," Roy said.

"It's a mile," Cammy whined.

"It's a quarter mile."

"Is a Ford a bad car?" Eric said.

"This one is," Roy said. "Come on. I need to loosen up this leg anyway."

The eastern sky paled. Crows cawed to one another across the fields; a late-arriving owl glided into the trees beyond the garbage pit. Eric saw the first bright leaves of pricker plants spreading among the wildflowers and prairie grass alongside the driveway. During walks the previous summer Aunt Phyl had identified many of the flowers. He still recognized the young rhubarb and the spray of leaves of stray corn that had blown over from the fields.

Cammy stopped and called back. "Does your leg hurt?"

"It's stiff, is all," Roy said. The cast had come off three days earlier. Putting his leg under the shower afterward ranked among the five most glorious moments of his life. The muscles refused to loosen, defied Phyl's vigorous applications of liniment, a surprise to Roy, considering she had loosened up a horse or two in her day. He found it hard to believe he would be able to climb back onto a roof come Monday morning.

Roy lit another cigarette. "What's your book, son?"

"It's about comets," Eric said. "I have to return it to the library."

"Didn't you go out looking for a comet during the winter?"

"Comet Kohoutek," Eric said.

"That's right."

They stopped at the end of the drive. Eric shaded his eyes to look for the bus. In his opinion he needed to catch a bus before seven like he needed a rash, but he conceded that getting up early helped with studying the universe. A lot seemed to happen in the hour before sunrise. Meteor showers intensified. The next season's constellations appeared like coming attractions. It was easy to find whichever planet served that day as the inaccurately named morning star. He hoped astronomers stayed up late. That he could do.

"There's the bus," Cammy exclaimed.

Cammy always worried the bus wouldn't come. Eric always worried it would. Since his mother died, he did not like to leave his father alone.

ROY DECLINED A DRAG off the offered joint.

"Breakfast of champions," Dombey said as he turned his car out of the long driveway.

After a minute Roy said, "How're things at the site?"

"All fucked up. Permit problem. That's why we're off today. You should've seen Gordon. That big ol' vein in his forehead popped out two inches this time. I hope I'm not standing in front of that fucker when it blows."

"At least it'd relieve the pressure."

"Grass is less messy," Dombey said. "So this thing I mentioned."

"Yeah?"

"You remember over weekends me and my brother-in-law were rehabbing that house for Gordon's old man?"

Roy nodded.

"He steered us to another guy. The Judge. That's what everyone calls him. Retired. Crazy as they come. Thinks the Army should put Nixon back in power if he gets impeached." Dombey let out a mouthful of smoke. "Got more money than he can spend so he collects stuff. His son—he was the one who hired us—his son told me about it. Civil War weapons. Watches. But the old man's big thing is coins. Dude's got a Roman coin. Somebody's head on it and everything. Older than Christ."

"Literally," Roy said.

"Worth a lot, too. Ought to be in a museum. Hell, maybe the Judge took it from one—someone told me he brought back some interesting stuff after the war. Anyway, he keeps it all in this room in his house. It's like a vault. Three locks, man. I guess when people come over he opens it up, gives a tour. So we had an accident and dented the wall. It's an old house. What we did jarred loose all the plaster. It was like breaking a mirror."

Roy had things to do, and Dombey never shut up so to move the story along he asked, "Do you need help fixing the wall?"

"Eventually." He paused to look over the joint. Not much was left. "We're gonna move some of the coins out. Just the best ones. No one'll know what's missing till the Judge gets home, and that's months away. I need someone to hide the stuff. If someone notices—the son, maybe—then the cops'll look at me because of my record. Once you're in the system, it's guilty until proven innocent. No one's gonna look at you, though. Kids. House. What happened with your wife."

"I think this is more than I want to hear," Roy said.

"Listen to me."

"Carl—"

Dombey lowered his voice. "It'll only take a week to move the stuff. The buyer's lined up already—we showed him Polaroids of the pieces, and he can't wait." He spoke over Roy's attempt to get a word in. "A third. You got all that space out there. Put a little bag somewhere for a week and you're in for a third. Five grand, maybe more."

"Come on," Roy said. "They'll be all over you."

"They won't know till fucking Christmas when the Judge comes back. My uncle thinks he might get twenty thousand out of the buyer once he sees the actual coin in his hand. A few thousand for him is like twenty bucks for you or me. It's all insured. The Judge won't be out a dollar. Meanwhile this coot we're selling to keeps the coins until he drops dead in five or ten years, then his kids sell the stuff, and the cops eventually catch up and seize the stuff as stolen goods. But the buyer's dead. Who's gonna answer their questions?"

"You'd go to prison for five thousand?" Roy replied.

"If we were talking about prison I wouldn't be doing it," Dombey said. "That's how sure I am. Are you saying you can't use five thousand bucks? You think we'll see any work from Gordon if the Arabs cut off the oil again? But this gives us a nice social safety net."

"Why don't you hide it?" he asked.

"I told you," Dombey said. "I got a record."

"This guy really wants to buy it?"

"He looked at those Polaroids like you and me look at center-folds. I thought he was gonna have an accident."

"What if he backs out?"

"He's not backing out."

"Entertain the thought," Roy said.

A smile parted Dombey's beard. "Then we put it all back and fix the wall."

"I don't have the guts. Sorry."

"That's the whole point of bringing you in," Dombey said, and he put a hand on Roy's arm. "Everyone knows you're honest. Hell, you could turn me down, and I know you'd still never say a word. I know it. That's why it's gonna work. That's why you're worth a share of the proceeds."

The excitement of the conversation had caused Dombey to speed up to about eighty. As he pulled a Marlboro from his pocket, they began to climb a hill.

"You want one?" he said.

"Sure."

They each used the car's lighter, and Dombey thumbed it back into the dash.

"Don't tell me no," he said. "Don't even tell me yes. Just think about it. I had to talk myself into it, too. But five, six, seven thousand, with what I owe? This car included? It wasn't much of a discussion."

The car reached the top of the hill. Roy knew the stretch of road. The far side of the hill smoothed out a short distance from a railroad crossing with lights but no gate. As they started down, Roy saw a long freight train snaking down the line from their right.

Dombey cut the engine. They began to coast.

"Carl," Roy said. "I'm not drunk enough to do this."

Momentum carried the car ahead. Without knowing it Roy gripped the underside of his seat with his free hand.

"Turn on the engine," he said.

Dombey began to sing the words to "Teen Angel."

"Goddamn it," Roy exclaimed.

But the singing went on. Roy tried to remain calm enough to calculate the speed of the train versus that of the car. On the hill he thought they had enough to get across with room to spare. But once they hit the short straightaway their speed began to die. The train was at medium speed but that was still too fast for it to stop. He asked Dombey, again and again, to start the engine, while at the same time he leaned forward, as if he that might coax more speed out of the car. The chimes from the crossing became louder than his voice, louder still. As they neared the tracks the engineer laid on the horn. Roy closed his eyes on the blunt nose of the locomotive.

The tires rumbled across the tracks. Behind them the train horn blasted away.

"Thirty yards," Dombey said as he restarted the engine. "Not even a record."

ON FRIDAY MORNINGS Eric's class fanned out into the library, leaving Miss Birch to chat with Mrs. Krakus, the head librarian. On his way back from the astronomy shelves Eric found Julie Garland playing with the library's fern. At her touch the plant closed its spines around her little finger. White-blond hair sprouted from elastic bands on either side of her head. She had to wear it this way because she refused to sit still for braids.

"What books are you checking out?" she asked and she cocked her head to study the spines. *Astronomy,* to be renewed for the thirteenth straight two-week period. On top of that was *Chariots of the Gods.*

"Are they for a book report?" Julie said.

"No," Eric said.

Julie held up *Chariots of the Gods.* "Is this about church?"

"It's about UFOs," Eric said.

"UFOs aren't real," Julie said.

"Your dad says they are. At baseball practice he told us about the time he saw one."

Julie frowned. "My mom says he's not suppose to tell that story."

They went to the checkout desk together. Mrs. Peterson put aside her stack of overdue slips. "Which one of you wants these books?"

"Him," Julie replied.

"Do you have any other books about comets?" Eric said.

"Check the card catalog, Eric," Mrs. Peterson said. "At least glance at the Dewey decimal system."

"We don't learn Dewey decimals until fourth grade," Julie said.

"Jenny—" Mrs. Peterson began.

"I'm Julie. Jenny's my sister."

"You're the Garland in fourth grade? Then show him the Dewey decimal system."

Julie led him to the stacks. "Jenny told me a better way than the Dewey decimals," she said in a low voice. "All the books on the same subject are put in one place. So where you found that book"—she pointed to *Astronomy*—"that's where the other astronomy books are."

"Don't you have to use the cards first?" Eric said.

"This way works better," Julie said.

"I mean, I thought that was the rule."

"I never use those dumb cards."

Eric was dubious. The teachers made the importance of the cards very clear. "So if I found one book about comets here," he said, trying to get it straight, "other books on comets will be here, too?"

"Yes," Julie said.

There were no new books on comets, then. He'd looked through every related book in the Nathan Hale library.

"Can you come over and play this weekend?" Julie asked.

"My aunt's coming from Chicago," Eric said.

"You can bring Cammy."

"Thanks. But I have to see my aunt."

Eric and Cammy had last spent an afternoon with the Garlands in September. It began with the Garland boys, Johnny and Tim, calling Cammy names, in whispers when they had to, in singsong when they could. Eventually they drove their sisters so wild with anger that toys were thrown. Cammy did her share of the shouting, too, but Eric felt humiliated, for his sister and himself, and confused to hear former teammates—teammates!—call Cammy a *retard*. The afternoon ended earlier than planned when Coach Garland overheard his sons. Eric had never witnessed a whipping like the one that followed. It was so bad he started crying himself. Upon hearing what happened, his mother forbade him to play at the Garlands again.

Eric stopped at the library door to scan the Answer Board. Two weeks before he had submitted a pair of questions. Why didn't Magellan pull off onto dry land to get food, instead of eating his boots? And did the Magellanic Clouds drift around in space the way Earth's clouds drifted through the sky? As usual the librarians answered queries other than his, explained instead the life cycle of silkworms and the reasons matches caught fire.

"They didn't answer," he said to Julie.

"You didn't ask about cancer again, did you?" Julie said.

The first cancer question landed him in the principal's office for a talk with Mr. Gray and the school nurse. By the end the school nurse was in tears. Eric, though unclear on why bad cells caused tumors, tried his hardest to make it clear he understood. He was distracted the whole time. Mr. Gray had called him in just before lunch, and Eric was hungry enough to eat his own shoes.

Eric and the rest of his class trailed Miss Birch back to the classroom. According to Julie, Miss Birch ironed her hair. Eric considered it possible, based on how straight it fell day after day. Thunder rumbled in the distance as they started in on English class. The storm had come closer by the time Miss Birch finished the poetry lesson and gave the class permission to "socialize." Eric and Joel Cramer, the kid who sat behind him, stared out the window. A green dome covered the sky from horizon to horizon. Miss Birch came over to have a look.

"I've never seen green before," she said.

"It probably means hail," Eric said.

Joel Cramer shook his head. "A yellow sky means hail."

"You have yellow skies, too?" Miss Birch said.

"And black," Eric said. "Maybe it means a tornado."

Miss Birch's lips—narrow, maroon, dry—twisted into a curlicue of worry.

"What do you do when a storm blows up?" she murmured.

"Go out on the porch to look at it," Joel said.

Miss Birch turned from the window. "Excuse me?"

"Unless there're sirens," Eric said.

"Right," Joel said. "Then my dad goes out, but we go to the basement."

By the time the bell rang patches of gray cloud had broken up the green. Miss Birch consulted for a moment with one of the older teachers and returned to say the buses were loading. During the rush for the door she called Eric's name and waved him to her desk.

She handed him a letter-sized envelope. "I want you to take this home."

"Okay," Eric said.

"You're not to open it."

"Okay."

"It's important. Don't forget."

A knot tightened in Eric's stomach.

"Have a good weekend," Miss Birch said.

He turned to go.

"Eric," she said.

"I will."

"Tie your shoe."

"I'll do it on the bus," he said.

The crash came five seconds later. Miss Birch reached the door in three long strides, saw that Eric had already gathered up his books. He hurried down the corridor, his shoelaces lashing the floor like live wires.

BY LATE MORNING ROY HAD the car and his heart running again. Phyl was busy cleaning the house and insisted he do the grocery shopping. She didn't want any comments from Deborah, she said, her teeth grinding over the name, as if it tested the deepest reserves of Southern graciousness. Roy said nothing. Ten years of marriage to Jean had taught him to stay out of the way when women fought for turf. Shopping allowed him to choose his lunches for the next week. Six weeks off had meant six weeks without deviled ham and garlic bologna, both of them long-time favorites, and often the sustenance of his married years amidst Jean's overdone round steaks and rubbery lima beans.

Cypress lacked a grocery store, so Roy drove eight miles to Sycamore. In the car he found the radio tuned to the oldies weekend show, an offshoot of *American Graffiti*'s popularity. Roy seldom listened. He shared Paul Le Mat's contempt for the Beach Boys and had heard enough of the Dave Clark Five the first time around. At the moment, however, all of the other pop and rock stations were playing ads, a pair of serious people discussed busing on the university's Progressive Underground FM station, and at all times he preferred the wind rushing through the window to the country and western he had grown up with in Missouri.

To his surprise he found the oldies palatable. Del Shannon's "Runaway" gave way to The Tokens, and The Tokens to a Lovin' Spoonful song that he had forgotten existed.

"'Darling Be Home Soon,'" Roy said to himself. The only Spoonful hit underplayed in its own time. As often happened with songs he'd forgotten, Roy could feel the lyrics and melody filling in the mental groove the song had created in . . . 1967? Was it '67? Yes. They were still measuring Eric's age in weeks instead of months. Roy worked in an appliance factory, Jean in an office.

They laughed more than they fought in those days. Nighttime brought comfort rather than dread of the next morning, and every morning brought promise, of a lucky break or a brilliant son, hell, of the Age of Aquarius, if that's what you wished for. A good time, worries about the draft aside, the best time, really, before Cammy's difficult birth and her string of illnesses, before all the moves in search of work, before Jean's college career added to the everyday stress and end-of-the-month shortfalls. That he forgot the song was no surprise, he thought. It had ceased to be relevant. In those days he could sincerely sing a line like "Darling be home soon" or a thousand others expressing love and lust and hope. Music then articulated his present and made him feel. Now it recalled the past and made him think.

He changed the station.

Soon after he pulled into the grocery store parking lot, took the wad of food stamps from the seat, and stuffed them into his pocket as he walked. Two gallons of milk went into the cart, and he wondered how much Cammy would sneak to the cats. The cookies, a lemon-flavored rip-off of Oreos, made him uneasy. So did the whole fryers. He tried to use the food stamps for essentials and cash for the rest. But cash was short. The fryers were on sale. And what kind of asshole begrudged kids a bag of cookies that tasted like furniture polish?

He did not know. But he felt their eyes on him as he emptied the cart.

Thinking about it reminded him of his last trip to the welfare office. Roy had met with a caseworker two weeks after breaking his leg. While he appreciated that she wished to help, he had a hard time getting past her appearance. She wore a sack dress and the largest turquoise necklace he'd ever seen on a woman under sixty. The knot of hair atop her head reminded him of Bert on *Sesame Street*.

"You said you eat out six times a month?" she had asked.

"Something like that."

"Your money will go further if you exchange those empty calories for an inexpensive substitute, like lentils."

"Lentils," Roy had said.

"They're an excellent source of protein and iron."

"My kids won't eat lentils."

She folded her hands. "They might if you set an example."

Roy had promised to give it a shot.

"If you must make hamburgers," the woman went on, "why not mix in bread crumbs to make the meat go further? Consider adding chopped onions and peppers to increase the meal's nutritional value." Then she brought out the chart with the five food groups.

The clerk counted out the food stamps without comment; but Roy stood with his face turned away from the farm wives and old ladies waiting behind him. By the time he got to the car his abdominal muscles hurt from being held so tight. On the way out of town he stopped at the liquor store to pick up cigarettes and a six-pack. Once a week, Eric asked Roy to buy the Schlitz tall boys with the wide, flat bottoms—for his project, he said, Eric obviously thinking he could put something past Phyl. Roy paused at the cooler, then laughed to himself. That damned kid, he thought. It took the advancement of scientific knowledge to make it worthwhile to drink piss like Schlitz.

At the counter Roy tossed a couple of packs of baseball cards next to the beer. The girls would want a treat, too, so he looked over the candy bars. Cammy ate sweets without discrimination. When it came to Grub, anything or nothing might do. Lately she lived on bread and frozen peas and refused everything else. A diet endorsed by social workers, maybe, but one that worried Phyl for nutritional reasons and Roy because it was weird.

The clerk handed him the bag. "Hope you get a Hank Aaron."

"It's for my son," Roy said.

"That's what they all say."

Static crackled under "The Loco-Motion" on the radio. Thus alerted Roy scanned the sky and noticed dark clouds to the west. As he neared Cypress he considered a stop at the tavern on the highway. It was less of a redneck joint in the afternoon.

And the grocery trip had shaken him up. To say nothin' of the fuckin' Lovin' Spoonful. And his kids were strange. And his wife was gone—

But it'd be a miserable weekend if Deb knew he'd spent an hour at a bar. Later that night he'd crack a couple of cans on the porch. He turned away from town, from the tavern. The knot in his stomach released a little and he felt a rush of pride, as with a job well done.

WHEN ERIC ENTERED THE KITCHEN his Aunt Deb stood next to the sink, holding Grub against her hip and talking about her drive. Five gallons of bottled water sat on the table. After suffering a kiss on the cheek, Eric pulled the milk from the refrigerator.

To his eye Aunt Deb looked like Mom in the face, but the differences were clearer. Aunt Deb's curly black hair, cut above the ears in a style Dad called "the Garfunkel," was nothing like the blond-red hippie haystack his mother had worn. Deb always showed up dressed in a suit or at least a skirt and blouse, never in Mom's flannel or blue jeans, certainly never in sandals.

"How was school?" she asked him.

"Okay," Eric said. "Your stomach's bigger."

"This is only the beginning. Emma weighed almost ten pounds."

Eric craned his neck to see around her. "Miss Birch gave me a letter, Dad."

"Well, hand it over," Roy said.

"I'm going outside," Eric said.

"Good idea, make a break for it."

Miss Birch had typed the note on official school district stationery.

April 26, 1974
Dear Mr. Conlon,

I am writing to request a meeting with you regarding Eric. You may recall that during our parent-teacher conference we discussed certain matters regarding his progress. I would like to follow up. He still spends a lot of time studying subjects other than the ones I'm trying to teach him, such as reading, math, and phonics.

Since we're coming to the end of the school year, I'd like to speak with you as soon as possible. Please call me at the school between 12 and 1 p.m., or at my home phone.

Sincerely yours,
Deidre Birch

Roy glanced at her number, then held the page to the light and noticed at least twenty whited-out mistakes. While Deb read the note he went to Eric's pile of books, as usual dropped on the kitchen table, and opened *Astronomy* to a random page. On the left he saw text and a picture of Sir William Herschel. On the right was a full-page photo of the Great Nebula, in Orion and in full color.

"What does she mean by 'subjects other than the ones I'm trying to teach him'?" Deb asked.

Roy stared into the pinks and purples of the nebula. Did other fathers look at their eight-year-old sons and suspect some unknowable inner person beyond the familiar exterior? Jean had claimed to understand Eric completely. Had she known where astronomy came from? His obsessive habits? Did she see into the part of him that was, always had been, a stranger to Roy?

"I don't know," he replied.

Deb folded the letter. "When are you going to see the teacher?"

"How I can see her? I'm building apartments in Byron all next week. I won't get home till after seven."

Eric listened through the kitchen window. Earlier in the year Miss Birch had caught him studying the same book instead of that day's reading assignment. He had caught hell. As he crept from the window he weighed the possibility he would catch more hell against having the book taken away *and* catching more hell.

PHYL OUTDID HERSELF with the accommodations. A knitted quilt covered the pullout bed in the tiny upstairs room Jean had called the study. Two pillows were centered beneath the single small window. Phyl had added a lamp and clock radio to the desk, recognizing that Deb always brought work or—Deb thought sourly—to encourage her to stay in the room.

The top two bookshelves along the opposite wall were stacked with Jean's old textbooks, relics of the college degree she had abandoned six hours short of completion. Deb flipped through one, saw the underlined passages, the dog-eared pages. Why had Jean never finished? Deb failed to recall her own conclusion from the time. At any rate it had been hard to parse out the truth with a woman who at any moment might drop all explanations and tell you to go to hell.

The bottom shelf held a mishmash of books Jean had picked up for the kids at Goodwill and garage sales—random *Encyclopaedia Britannica* volumes, field guides to insects and mammals and nonflowering plants, *Betty Crocker's Cooky Book,* a battered *Guinness Book of World Records 1971.* But someone had removed photos from the third shelf—Jean's high school picture and a more recent shot with Roy. The kids' school photos remained, as did one of Roy's mother and two of the dog.

Deb finished unpacking and went downstairs to call her husband. Fergus was attending a department cocktail party that evening, and she'd be long asleep by the time he got home. When she picked up the phone, she heard a man speaking in a 45-record-played-at-33 sort of voice.

"Doctor says it must be trouble with stones," he said.

The party line, Deb thought, aghast.

A younger woman replied, "Are you sure he didn't say *bones*?"

"Stones. Definitely stones."

"What'd he say next?"

"Might have to have surgery," the man said. "Have to take painkillers."

"You'd want the painkillers," the woman said.

The man made a snorting noise. "So's I get hooked on the dope?" Deb eased the phone back into the cradle. At that moment Grub staggered up to her and said, "Hungry."

"Roy," Deb called, "your children are hungry."

"I'm going to grill," he said from the yard. "There's hamburger thawing in the sink. Could you pat them out?"

"What do you want to serve with it?"

"Ask the kids."

She leaned out of the kitchen and asked.

"Corn," Eric said.

"Peas," Grub said.

"Is she still living on peas?" Deb said.

"And white bread," Cammy replied.

"Aunt Phyl says it's a miracle she's alive," Eric said.

Phyl and I agree on something, Deb thought.

"What about some peanut butter and bananas, honey?" Deb asked. Grub shook her head, first to the peanut butter and bananas, then to each individually, and then to everything else visible in the kitchen. After Grub returned to the TV with her slice of white bread, Deb went out onto the porch. Roy was lavishing lighter fluid over charcoal.

"For your information," Deb said, "your daughter's going to starve to death."

"You'd think so," Roy said, "but she keeps growing."

Shadows fell across the yard. Looking up, Deb said, "Are you sure it won't rain?"

"I've got my fingers crossed," Roy said.

The motto these people live by, she thought.

ERIC SIGNED UP FOR BASEBALL on Saturday morning. Playing the previous season had whittled his daydreams from being Reggie Jackson to escaping right field. In twelve games he had four balls hit in his direction, and two of those over his head. Worse, his midgame replacement was Ed Arndt, one of Cammy's classmates from special education. Whatever his handicaps, Ed Arndt—as with Charlie Brown, people always used his full name—played with style. His flip-up sunglasses were the envy of the league. Unfortunately, he paid more attention to the shades than to fly balls, so Mrs. Arndt insisted he wear a helmet in the outfield. This only added to his mystique. Failure did not faze Ed Arndt. No chatter shook him and no situation daunted him, whereas Eric cried after his strikeouts, especially when he made all three outs in an inning. Ed Arndt had hit four fair balls during the season and scored at least twice.

"Will I be on the same team as last year?" Eric asked.

"I think so," Roy said. "They organize teams by where you live."

Being teammates with Johnny Garland, the league's best pitcher, guaranteed Eric another first place trophy. It also meant three months of being knocked on his behind during stolen-base drills, of watching Johnny stomp and scream himself red-faced over balls and strikes, of receiving personal threats if—in Eric's case, when—you made a mistake.

Lorraine Garland leapt up from her chair behind the registration table, took Eric's face in her hands, made the usual fuss. Roy filled out the forms while Mrs. Garland held up shirts to Eric's chest. Numbers one and two were reserved for the team's new players, both of them second graders.

"I think number three will fit," Mrs. Garland said. "Are you looking forward to baseball?"

"Yes," Eric lied.

"I'm sure you'll do great, sweetie. You got so much better last year. How are your sisters?" Eric winced as she yanked the stiff new hat over his eyes. "Well, that's the best we can do. Now what are you up to today?"

"The garden," Eric said.

"We rented a rototiller," Roy added.

"That's just wonderful," Mrs. Garland said. "You should be fine, just fine. We won't have another hard frost, I don't think. Eric, sweetie, it looks like you're ready. Don't lose your hat, because we don't have any extras."

They returned home to their work, Eric to his room, his father to the garden. Roy, unable to hear above the roar of the rototiller, failed to notice the landlady's car. Only when he caught sight of Eric waving his arms did Roy cut the engine and put on his shirt. The landlady was waiting in the car, dressed in black, looking like a mourner impatient to put a hated husband to rest. Her son, the man who farmed the surrounding farmland, helped her out of the car. She then shook off his arm to hobble over on her own.

"Where is the rent?" she said.

Roy knew every reason would sound like an excuse to her. Every reason sounded like an excuse to him.

"I'm a little short," he answered.

"If money's so short why's the pit full of beer cans? Do you remember you signed a lease? Using your wife as an excuse has gone on long enough, hasn't it?"

"Mother," her son sighed.

"Have you started work yet?" she said.

"I just started back full time," Roy said.

"I thought you got that cast off weeks ago."

The rototiller had dulled Roy's hearing enough so that when he looked at the ground he could almost block out the rest of it. Almost. Three kids and this was the example he set. How many months late did he plan to be? An immigrant she knew from church, just off the plane from Iran, had already earned enough to buy a house. That's hard work. People from other countries were the only ones that appreciated America anymore.

"I'll have it Wednesday," he said when she stopped.

The landlady jabbed a finger at him. "I'll be here. And I want to see what you've been doing to my house. If it's damaged I'll throw you out. Don't think I won't."

Her son tried to seem stony but the red in his face gave him away. Roy, out of courtesy, made sure not to look at him.

Eric watched from the kitchen window as the landlady whipped her car around and, with an indignant spewing of gravel, drove down the driveway. The burning in his cheeks subsided as the engine's noise died away, replaced again by the birds, and the crickets chirping away from under the porch. When Roy started toward the house Eric slid off the stool and slipped up the stairs to his bedroom.

"Eric?" Roy called.

"Up here," Eric said.

"Where'd Aunt Deb go?"

"She took the girls to get haircuts."

"Why didn't she take you, too? Come out here and start breaking up these clots."

Eric did not want to see him. "I'll be out in a minute. Aunt Deb said to clean my room."

Eric retrieved the grease pencil from his pencil box, wedged the tomato sauce can tight between his feet, and for the sixth time attempted to draw Scorpius, the Scorpion. On his father's suggestion he always started in the center of the constellation, to keep the outlying stars from spilling off the edges of the can. In the center of Scorpius shone the red supergiant Antares—*Al Kalb* "the heart," to the Arabs—one of the legendary stars in the sky and, like the constellation itself, an object Eric could find without referring to a book. The Egyptians and Greeks had built temples that lined up with Antares on the equinoxes. Once, to get Aunt Phyl going, Eric suggested *all* churches be built that way. Aunt Phyl said Billy Graham considered that using-the-stars-to-predict-the-future business to be the work of the Devil. She didn't get the difference between astronomy and astrology.

Eric checked the illustration in *Stars* several times before making the first mark. The next star up—that is, toward the Scorpion's claws—went awry. He wiped the errant grease with his thumb. He'd already spent three of the cans brought by Aunt Deb trying to get it right. But he kept mismatching the size of the nail holes to the varying magnitudes illustrated in the book. When he got one reasonably accurate, he ruined it by trying to add the nearby star clusters. With that many holes he'd have a watering can instead of a constellation.

Three more misplaced stars and Eric smashed the can with his foot. He immediately thought: That was stupid. He picked up the can, saw the open top bent into a writhing frown. All the ruined scorpions went into a paper grocery bag—this passed for cleaning his room—and he finally plodded outside to the garden.

Roy was allowing Mr. Johnson a drink to drink from the hose. Eric recalled that egg water did not bother dogs.

"You ready to work?" Roy said.

"Cleaning my room was work," Eric said.

"Well, get ready for more. Do you have any idea what you want to plant?"

"I only like watermelons and cantaloupes."

"Aunt Phyl asked us to plant collard greens," Roy said. "Don't let me forget."

"Grub would like peas, I bet."

"Okay, that's a start. We'll go buy seeds tomorrow. Is that old radio sitting in the kitchen window?"

"Aunt Phyl has it on the preacher station," Eric said.

"Maybe I'll change it," Roy said as he started toward the house. "Be careful with that hoe, son. Choke up on it and watch your feet."

Eric called, "Do we need money for the landlady?"

"It's a misunderstanding," Roy said. "Don't worry about it."

"We can make money selling the vegetables so Aunt Phyl won't make them for supper," Eric said.

"Nice try."

At first they worked without speaking. Eric gave up the hoe in favor of breaking the clots with his feet. A string of radio ads gave way to the jingle, and the jingle to the DJ talking up the next song, "Clap for the Wolfman," by The Guess Who. During the chorus—punctuated by actual jive from the Wolfman—Eric let loose with his Wolfman Jack voice, much practiced on the playground even if boggling to his classmates. Roy laughed.

"Do you even know who the Wolfman is?" he asked.

"He's on TV," Eric said. "When you worked nights, I used to see him when me and Mom waited up for you."

"Oh, on *The Midnight Special*."

"The Wolfman tells you who the singers are," Eric said. "He really digs them, baby, HAHAHA."

Roy had scouted out the place when looking for reasons to avoid going home. It was a short walk from the road, though the lack of path made it harder going; and while the fishing was no better than anywhere else, the sheltered location spared him the advice of the regulars. Others had used it, however. Chalked scrawls of graffiti had faded on the rock shelf jutting out from the bank, and nearby someone had driven a metal tent stake still wrapped with a loop of narrow rope. Eric tugged on it.

"Don't do that, son," Roy said.

"Why?"

"Because it'll give and you'll fall in the water."

I have to get someone to teach him to swim, Roy added to himself.

"Can I use a fly?" Eric asked.

"I brought chicken livers."

Roy began to bait the hooks. Eric pointed to them.

"Johnny Garland stuck one of those in his finger once," he said.

"That doesn't surprise me," Roy said.

"He said it hurt worse than the time the baseball hit him in the crotch."

"I caught one in the ear once when I was casting. I must've been a year or so older than you. A friend of mine had to dig it out with a jackknife." Then it occurred to Roy that it was the wrong time for the story. True enough, the queasy look on Eric's face told him all he needed to know about his son's willingness to cast today. Instead Roy let out a length of the line and gave the hook and bobber an easy toss. Roy passed over the rod. Eric, as he always did, handled it like glass. They quietly talked over the usual topics, why fish disliked loud noise and what species lived in the water.

When twenty minutes had passed Eric said, "Should we throw the lines out where it's deeper?"

"It's pretty deep here," Roy said, motioning to the left off the rock shelf. "For some reason the river bottom drops off sharply right under us. I even saw a few big bass not far from where you're sitting."

Someone called Roy's name. A figure approached, stiffly stepped over a fallen tree, and joined them in the clearing. A riot of brown hair crowned a head made long by the man's massive jaw. Pink grooves bracketed the top of his nose. Cowell wore a plaid shirt and faded jeans held up by a studded belt. His work boots were stained with all the fluids found in a cars and trucks and helicopters. He hadn't shaved in three or four days and as usual he smelled of oil.

"Hi," Eric said.

"Hi yourself," Cowell said. "I was passing by and saw your car up top. Having any luck?"

"Not yet," Roy said.

"You work on Saturdays?" Eric asked.

"Yeah, buddy," Cowell said. "They're so behind at that place they'd have me in on Sundays, except they know Phyl'd be down there reading them the Fourth Commandment. The weatherman's saying storms later, too, so I'll be out watching the clouds for the sheriff."

"You're a policeman now?"

"An auxiliary deputy, or maybe it's a deputy auxiliary." He turned to Roy. "They have to give out a nice title since it's all volunteers. Can I get a drag of that cigarette? Don't go telling on me to your Aunt Phyl," he added to Eric.

"I won't," Eric said.

"I may need you to look at the engine again," Roy said.

"Phyl told me it was acting up," Cowell said. "I'll bring over some incense and candles. We'll get her going again. Speaking of going—I better so's I can get some food in me. How's your leg?"

"Stiff. About what I expected."

Cowell looked away, pretended interest in the bobbers as he asked, "You okay otherwise?"

He meant financially.

"Yeah," Roy said.

"Good enough," Cowell said, and he stood. "Eric, you catch a talking fish, make sure he gives you three wishes."

"Why do you always say that?" Eric asked.

"Because it's only chance I have of getting rich," Cowell said, and he sighed.

"I'LL HAVE TO CLEAR IT WITH FERGUS," Deb said. "Can you ask your sister?"

Roy's voice barely registered. "I already owe Phyl money."

"I don't anticipate a problem," Deb said. Just the opposite, she thought. Neither new mortgage nor oncoming infant would dissuade her husband from helping. He already contributed to an expanding legion of Girl Scouts, undergrads, acid casualties, down-and-out vets, and Hare Krishnas. "Before you go," she added, "I stopped by Phyllis's house to thank her for making up the room. To try to bury the hatchet, to be frank. It didn't work. I get the idea she thinks I'm a know-it-all."

Roy said nothing.

"She pointed out that Cammy has a couple of teeth coming through the upper part of her gums," Deb went on. "Above and over the baby teeth. Did you know that?"

He lit a cigarette, shook out the match. "I thought it'd correct itself when her baby teeth fell out."

"The lack of fluoridated water isn't helping."

"What am I supposed to do?"

"Peruvians live this way, Roy. Can't you find another house?"

"I pump drinking water at the park," he said. "Spring water's good for you."

"It still doesn't have fluoride. I realize the Birchers think fluoride is a communist mind-control plot, but you understand why we put it in the water, right? Please take milk containers or whatever you've got to Phyllis's and fill them up."

"Sometimes I do," Roy said.

"Why sometimes?"

He shrugged.

"You have to take care of this," Deb exclaimed.

Roy waved her off. "What I really have to do is go. I'm late."

"Are you going to call Eric's teacher?" Deb asked.

"I already did."

"When?"

"The other night. Christ."

"Can I go with you to the meeting?"

"Whatever you want, Deb."

Roy walked into the morning sunlight. Not long after, Eric stumbled down the stairs. When he arrived in the kitchen, Deb pushed buttered toast and a glass of milk at him.

"Let me see your teeth," she said.

Eric gave the fake smile usual with that request.

"Do they ever hurt?" Deb asked.

"When they're loose," he said. "My baby teeth are all gone now. I might get my teeth pulled for money. Like Granny had her teeth pulled, except I wouldn't do it for dentures. When the Tooth Fairy comes I'll have a whole pile of quarters."

"You don't believe in the Tooth Fairy," Deb said.

"No, but I still get a quarter when I lose a tooth."

"What'll you do without teeth?"

"If I don't have to brush them I can sleep later," Eric said, biting off more toast.

"Go to bed earlier," Deb said.

"It's hard in the spring and summer. The days are longer so I have to stay up later, until it gets dark, to use my telescope. Dad lets me sometimes. Not Aunt Phyl. She says I'm ruining my eyes."

The next afternoon Eric arrived home from school and headed straight to the garden. Not a sprout had appeared in the forty-eight long hours since they'd planted. The only change was that the wind had blown over the signs at the end of the rows. He picked up the narrow strip of plywood with the leeks package on the end. The same thing had happened the year before. Stronger materials were available, but Eric could not convince his father to saw up the broomsticks.

Aunt Deb came into the yard, dressed in the formal clothes she'd worn when she arrived. "I'm going to leave for home after the meeting with your teacher," she said.

"Late at night?" Eric said.

"It's only ninety minutes back to the city."

"Are you going home to have the baby?"

"Good god, no," Deb said. "I'll be the size of your barn before that happens."

"When will you come back?"

"Once my school year ends, assuming the Registrar's Office didn't burn to the ground in my absence. I'll have more time then and I can stay longer."

On her command Eric gave her a hug and endured kisses on the cheek. The station wagon sputtered and knocked, and Aunt Deb tore off in a cloud of dust. As he passed through the kitchen he saw Aunt Phyl stirring a pot of his dad's ham and beans. The radio over the sink talked about Jesus.

Eric went into the guest room. The odor of Aunt Deb's soap and perfume hung in the air. He sat down, back against the bed, and drew out a stack of records from next to the bookshelf. These were the kids' albums and exiles from the adults' collection; Eric had standing permission to play them as much as he wanted on the room's old stereo. John Denver had, with Deb's help, made his way to the front of the pile. A dangerous state of affairs. If Cammy found the album it meant weeks of "Annie's Song." The rest of the albums appeared in the usual order, his mother's Andy Williams and Neil Diamond and, last in the stack, the family's copy of *Tapestry*.

According to his father, everyone on Earth owned this album, with the possible exception of Aunt Phyl. Eric considered the album cover "totally crazy," as the Wolfman might say. For one thing he liked the way the singer looked, with her crazy curly hair and blue jeans and bare feet. For another, the picture suggested several mysteries. Did everyone in New York City live in an apartment? From what he'd seen on TV shows, Eric assumed New York lacked houses as he understood them. What was the cat's name? What was with those pictures of Carole King knitting on the inside sleeve? Eric had considered writing her a letter. Over the winter he and several classmates had, with Miss Birch's help, written a letter to another famous person—E. B. White, the author of *Stuart Little*. Unlike White, Carole King might actually answer. Did kids write her letters? Did she even like kids? His father thought she had a daughter, so probably she did.

Eric removed the album. As instructed by his father he balanced the disk between the palms of his hands before loading it onto the turntable. He sat back to listen, or rather to remember his mother lounging in bare feet screeching along with the lyrics, or swearing at the sewing machine because it foiled her dressmaking ambitions, or chasing Dusty off the bed on one of the rare occasions he emerged from behind the refrigerator, asking why they bought the damn cat anyway, forgetting she had bought Dusty, and named him, and turned against him.

He could remember the events. But it was getting harder to see them in his mind.

"Eric?" Aunt Phyl called up.

"Eric is gone," he said.

She gave one of her grunts. "Get him back here to mix up the lemonade."

ROY THOUGHT THAT Nathan Hale Elementary—a.k.a. Nathan Jail—smelled like all of Eric's other schools. Maybe all schools, period. Kids, like dogs, might give off any odor at a given moment, but Roy was amazed by the combination of old textbooks, floor wax, finger paint, and cafeteria emissions that inevitably overpowered the array of things students stepped in, ran through, ate, drank, and produced by natural processes.

Deb knocked on the open classroom door and impatiently waved Roy forward. Hands were shaken. Having forgotten most of the parent-teacher conference, Roy was surprised to see that Miss Birch—he knew her only as Eric knew her—stood close to six feet tall. She parted her hair with a surveyor's perfection and tonight wore it in the kind of ponytail Roy associated with high school girls.

They sat in chairs borrowed from the teacher's lounge. "Try to ignore the holes from the cigarettes," Miss Birch said. Deb laughed politely. Roy craved a smoke.

Deb motioned to Miss Birch's red sweatshirt. "You went to Wisconsin?"

"The People's Republic," Miss Birch replied with a nervous laugh.

"I'm an administrator at UIC," Deb said. "Did you like Madison?"

"Yes. But I only went for my Master's, so I escaped full indoctrination."

Roy tried to imagine Miss Birch smoking grass or chanting chants. From the looks of her he guessed it more likely she'd spent Friday nights at the library and worked off her vegetarian meals worrying about the dean's list.

Deb folded her hands in her lap and from the summit of her rigid posture asked, "So how is Eric doing?"

"Very well," Miss Birch said. "As I told Mr. Conlon during parent-teacher conferences,"—she glanced at Roy,—"Eric is a bright, motivated student. Sometimes he's too interested in what he wants to learn and not interested enough in what I want to teach him." She stretched a gangly arm and took a worn paperback off her desk. "Please return this to him," she said, handing Roy the library's copy of *Chariots of the Gods.* "He was reading it during phonics today. Boys go through a flying saucer phase now. With my brothers it was dinosaurs."

"You take it in good humor," Deb said, as she improved her posture even more.

Roy thought, Please don't eat the poor girl alive.

Miss Birch turned more formal in response. "Reading I can handle. In my experience, bored children don't usually choose books as an alternative." She turned to Roy. "I have a question. Eric attended the Akhmatova School. What did you think of it?"

As far as Roy knew, his wife sent Eric to Akhmatova because she had admired the teachers and administrators she met in her education classes. Since Cammy went to a special school, it made sense to send Eric to one aimed at children at the other end of the spectrum. Or that was Roy's opinion—Jean would never admit to that kind of calculation, nor allow the suggestion Cammy could be anything less than the Leonardo da Vinci of the special needs set.

Akhmatova's rules required every parent to observe the class once. Roy had no idea what to make of it. The team of four teachers looked like the staff of a used record store—lots of denim and hair, no shortage of beads and ankhs, either. They ran around checking on groups of kids, at times herding a pod across the hall to the library, say, or into the corner of the room set up like a temple to arithmetic. During his visit Roy watched one of them plop down with a guitar and start strumming the chords to "Suzy Q." That an educator would play such a dumb-ass song offended Roy far more than the intrusion of music into the school day. According to Eric, it was the most played song by far. This did not raise Roy's opinion of the place.

"It was unusual," Roy answered.

"Yes," Miss Birch said, smiling.

"My wife liked that the kids learned at their own pace."

"Did you agree?"

"Eric seemed to get a lot out of it," Roy said. He felt suddenly self-conscious of the sawdust on his shirt. His desire for a cigarette proceeded from craving to torment. "I didn't know much about the theories that are, you know, behind the place, but my wife thought it was worth a try."

"She strongly believed in the ideas underlying the methods at the school," Deb added.

Miss Birch paused for a reply. Roy felt the urge to argue, but more than anything he wanted to get on with this conversation so they could go home and Miss Birch could get some dinner—much needed, by the looks of her, maybe as much as he needed a smoke.

"I took the liberty of calling Ruth Schultz," Miss Birch said.

"She was the ringleader of the teachers," Roy said to Deb.

"That's a good way of putting it," Miss Birch said. "Ruth told me an interesting anecdote. Akhmatova has a tradition. If a student is transferring or leaving the school, they let him or her do whatever he or she likes on the last day. Judging from my class, I doubt most students do much. Eric spent the afternoon trying to get as far as possible in math. Akhmatova uses a math program organized into levels, and he was determined to get to Level Four. Did you know that?"

"He never mentioned it," Roy said.

"Pardon me," Deb said, "but are you suggesting Eric is exceptional in some way?"

"I'm not sure I'd say exceptional in the way educators use the term," Miss Birch said. "What's unusual is his level of motivation—his ability to go into this other place, this sort of trance, when he does certain kinds of work, if you know what I mean. I've heard him trying to sound out Latin and Arabic words in the library. Related to astronomy, of course. In fact, he's asked me to help him. His single-mindedness is not what I'm used to. I wish some of my other students could keep their minds on anything for five minutes."

Deb cleared her throat. "Was he like this before his mother's death?"

"He was. And Ruth Schultz remembers him in the same way. A story, if you don't mind. My brother began to paint when he was about five. He wasn't Picasso as a child—Bobby's not a genius, and he bothered to learn to read and write—but he spent ungodly amounts of time, on his own, drawing and painting. At one point he designed a zoo—the buildings, the habitats, the murals. These balsa wood buildings took up half his room. Anyway, years later we moved to California. My mother took him to enroll at the high school, and Bobby asked to take the school's art classes. He'd already aced the same classes at his previous school, but he wanted to get new opinions on his work. Of course, this violated the school's rules, so instead of encouraging his enthusiasm, this idiot of a guidance counselor forced him to take electives of no interest to him whatsoever. He did fine. He's smart. But it didn't help him get to where he knew he wanted to go."

"What does your brother do now?" Deb asked.

"He paints."

Roy looked around the classroom. "I guess they wouldn't teach astronomy here."

"Astronomy may be a phase," Miss Birch said. "Like dinosaurs. But any encouragement for learning, a respect for it, goes a long way. I mean, if Eric showed an unusual precocity for football, wouldn't you consider hiring a coach to work with him?"

"Let me just ask," Roy said. "I get what you're saying, it's good in a way, but is it normal?"

"Is what normal?" Miss Birch said.

"Focusing on one thing the way he does."

"I doubt there's a working concert pianist who started later than his age," Miss Birch added. "Or many quarterbacks, either. While there are children forced into those pursuits, for many of them, it comes from inside. They find some calling—for want of a better word—and it takes them away. You don't have to ask them to practice, you have to stop them and send them outside. I'm sure there's research on why it happens. An encouraging environment, the confidence that comes with having a knack for something, following in a parent's footsteps—things like that. But

I believe there are cases when it's a mystery. Are you interested in astronomy, Mr. Conlon?"

He had to laugh. "Not at all."

"So who knows, right?"

"He is definitely into it," Roy replied, unsure of what else to say, trying to sound proud.

"Very much so," Miss Birch said. "He gave a valentine to Elise Stregnow. On it he wrote, 'If you add a C and a P, your name spells eclipse.'"

PHYL HAD A POT OF HAM and beans on the stove and a Billy Graham rerun on the radio. The landlady had called to remind him of her visit, she said. Roy grunted. Before he could get to the bathroom, however, Phyl pointed at the floor to his left.

"Looks like a leak," she said.

Roy vaguely recalled hearing a dripping sound the previous week. Weeks. He'd completely forgotten. Water had warped a section of the floor as big around as the dining room table. Kneeling, he ran a thumb over the black stains in the cracks, pushed down on boards that had twisted into a sharp W and brought up the nearby floorboard.

Phyl joined him, drying her hands on a towel. "Is it bad?"

He had experience installing hardwood floors. Not a lot, but enough to know it would take him ten days to put down a new floor and allow the glue to dry.

"I should've checked it," Roy said. "Going back to work—I forgot."

"It's just part of it."

"The whole floor has to be replaced, Phyl."

"Well, you can't fix it tonight," she said.

But Roy hadn't heard. "You can never match up new wood to the old wood," he exclaimed. "Jesus Christ. It'll be hundreds of dollars even if I do the work myself. She wants to evict us already, and now the floor's warped."

Phyl interrupted him. "Don't worry about that yet. The first thing to do is hide it from the old heifer."

The damage had been done in an area between the bottom of the stairs and the bathroom—moving a table there would announce something was wrong. Phyl thought of alternatives as Roy ranted. By the time she had a winner Eric and Cammy had crept to the top of the stairs. She stared them down until they retreated to bed.

"Those boxes you packed," Phyl said.

"What boxes?" He turned to her. "Jean's stuff?"

"That's right. You can say you're putting them in storage. That's about half-true. Stack them up all over. She won't know the difference. Once she's gone we can give you what you need to fix it up."

Deflated, Roy said, "I can't take more money from you."

"You're my people, aren't you? Listen to me, now. I don't hate money. I think that kind of attitude is communism. But I don't love it, either. That's from the Bible, Roy. I won't give you chapter and verse since it just makes you roll your eyes, but the idea's in there, more times than just about anything else. Giving a little to you doesn't stop me from buying what I need. It also keeps me from wanting more or getting proud—and there's no sin deadlier than pride."

He tried to protest but the argument ended, for the moment, with Phyl readying herself for the drive home. When she had gone Roy began moving the boxes from his bedroom. He covered all the damage and even managed to make the stacks look natural. This labor on top of the fatigue from the workday caused his leg to throb. He washed down a few aspirin with a beer. On his way to bed he looked over the boxes and thought: What if the kids dig into them? Roy didn't think they could handle seeing Jean's blouses and slacks and dresses. He couldn't, either. Not again. Not when it had taken most of a case of Olympia to get the stuff in the boxes.

WITH ROY BACK AT WORK, Eric and Cammy walked to Aunt Phyl's house after school. Few of Eric's friends lived in town so he usually passed the time enjoying Phyl's superior TV reception or talking to her in her garden. Eric admired the flair for decoration that led Aunt Phyl to encourage her tomato vines to infiltrate a pair of old lattice shutters Uncle Cowell had bought for a quarter each at an estate sale and, out of respect for Midwest storms, had hammered three inches into the ground. Her carrots and peas grew in precise lines. Bunches of azaleas rounded off the garden's corners. When Eric asked to plant flowers, Roy insisted they were too hard to grow. His request for a trellis only elicited a sigh. "You could make one with your tools," Eric had insisted. "You're good at finding me work to do," Roy replied.

Uncle Cowell arrived driving a blue number Eric had never seen before. At any given time Cowell and Phyl owned at least three vehicles—his pickup, her burnt-orange station wagon, and whatever car (or cars) he happened to be repairing, sometimes for resale and sometimes as a favor.

A few minutes later he joined Eric on the porch, a glass of iced tea in his hand. "What're you doing out here?" he said in his scratchy voice.

"Watching the sky," Eric said.

"It's fixing to storm. Don't need a weatherman to know which the wind blows. Hold this for me."

He handed Eric the iced tea and lit up a cigarette. Then he reached into his shirt pocket and traded the contents for the glass.

"It's a harmonica," Eric said, turning it over in his hand. "Harcerz, Made in Poland" was engraved on both sides.

"Call it a harp," Cowell said.

"I know what a harp is. This is a harmonica."

"Here I get you something, and you're sassing me. Listen. This is a different kind of harp. Over the weekend I found a box of them at a garage sale. Bought them all for two bucks. I don't see many curved like that one. Give it a try."

Eric blasted away.

"It tastes like wood," he said.

"Just what I thought myself," Cowell said. "You can see the middle piece there is wood. I didn't know they played harp in Poland. Fellas must do it when they can't afford an accordion."

Phyl put a bowl of popcorn between them. The wind rolled a few kernels across the porch. Cowell tilted his head back and dropped several pieces into his mouth in a slow cascade. Eric watched in admiration, but kept to eating two or three pieces at a time.

"When did you learn to play the harmonica?" Eric said.

"Back when I was little, like you," Cowell said as he chewed. "I learned more in the Navy."

"Did you go on boats?"

"I fixed engines, same as I do now. At first I worked on trucks, then I started on helicopters later on."

"Was the Navy fun?" Eric said.

Cowell smiled through the cigarette smoke. "Okay, I guess. It's hard to have real fun in the Navy, though."

"Did you ever get marooned?"

"What makes you ask that?" Cowell said.

"I read about Magellan," Eric said. "He was an explorer."

"Mmm."

"When he was going around the world, his ship got stuck because the wind wouldn't blow. He ran out of food, and the sailors on the ship had to eat their boots. Why didn't he take the boat close to the land and find food?"

"There's no telling with officers," Cowell said.

Aunt Phyl came to the door. For a moment Uncle Cowell huddled with her through the screen. Eric pretended interest in the harmonica but heard her mutter, "He should be done with the landlady by now." A moment later Cowell sat down next to him with a groan, swirled the ice around his glass.

"What kind of car is that?" Eric asked.

"A '68 Chevy Nova," Cowell said. "Close to seventy thousand miles, though—they must've driven it to Alaska a few times. She runs good, but I'm worried about some of that rust."

"Are you going to keep it?"

"A hot rod like that? I'll sell her to some high school kid with too much money."

Eric looked down the block, toward the highway. "I know what a nova is."

"Me, too," Cowell said. "It's a car."

Aunt Phyl began to chop up the chicken to fry. Through the *thok-thok-thok* of her knife Eric heard the TV announce severe weather watches. He mouthed along with the list of counties: Carroll, Ogle, Lee, DeKalb, Whiteside, Grundy, Winnebago, Boone. The storm system was so dangerous it rated a special appearance by the weatherman. He warned everyone in the viewing audience to remember the Xenia, Ohio, tornadoes of the month before, how those were only part of a huge outbreak that struck thirteen states and lower Canada. Eric returned to the window, watching the racing clouds and the corner at the end of the street, one after the other.

When Aunt Phyl told Eric to set the table, Cowell said, "Wait for Roy another minute."

"These children won't starve at my house," Aunt Phyl said.

Cowell joined her in the kitchen. Eric strained his ears to pick out words from the hiss of their voices. A minute later, Cowell returned to the living room looking defeated. To Eric's quizzical look he said, "Better get on it, sailor."

The kids picked at their food. So did Phyl. That told Cowell he was in for a long night, not that it ruined his appetite. He finished two helpings and much of the kids' food besides.

Cowell began to feel anxious when the minute hand rounded seven thirty. He left every morning at five thirty to get to O'Hare on time. To make the schedule work, he seldom stayed up past nine o'clock. That would be a hard deadline to meet with an APB out on Roy and the kids stranded in his living room. Grub was out cold on the sofa, but Cammy kept asking about her father, and Phyl's answers had deteriorated from "He'll be here any minute" to an "I don't know" delivered through grinding teeth. Eric did his homework in the next room and said nothing at all. Cowell went onto the porch to watch the ominous sky. Lightning caused the approaching thunderheads to glow pink here, white there. A short night to be sure. Even if Roy rolled up in the next sixty seconds the sheriff might call out the storm-watchers at any moment. And Roy wasn't going to roll up in the next sixty seconds.

When Cowell felt Phyl coming toward the screen door he figured it was best to get started on the inevitable. "You mind getting my jacket?" he asked.

"Do you know where he is?" Phyl said.

"I reckon I can hit it in three guesses."

"I'm going to run the kids home."

"That's good. I'll meet up with you there."

Cowell took the Nova on a courtesy drive past Cooper's, though he knew Roy disliked the place, as he disliked all rednecky places. No sign of his car. On the outskirts of DeKalb he spotted Roy's Ford parked outside Stan's Tap Room. If nothing else Roy had sense enough to go where he was known. At the door Cowell heard a woman laughing and the crack of balls on the pool table. The patron on the stool at the end of the bar gave him a sour look.

"Goddamn, Buddha, you'd think I was your ex-wife," Cowell said.

"You know, your brother-in-law's a real asshole," Buddha said, more dispirited than angry.

Cowell tossed two dollars onto the bar. "Have a couple more. Where's my asshole brother-in-law now?"

"Sleeping it off in his car. Stan had him carried out."

Buddha paused, as if unsure about whether to go on. Having never known Buddha Brenner to withhold a complaint, Cowell feigned interest in the television and waited.

"He lit out after me," Buddha finally said. "Insulted me."

"What'd old boy say?"

"He called me fat."

"You are fat," Cowell exclaimed. "You're sitting on every side of that stool but the bottom."

Buddha looked sullen. "It wasn't good-natured."

"Never mind Roy," Cowell scoffed. "You know what he's been through."

"That's no excuse. That's just no excuse."

The bartender approached. He was tall and pear-shaped, with an Amish-style beard and a belt buckle made out of buffalo nickels.

"What's the damage, Stan?" Cowell said.

"Nothing," Stan said. "A few bad names, nothing too original. This isn't the first time, Cowell. If he wants to start an altercation, he can come in on the weekends when I've got help. Tell him if this continues, I'll ban him."

"I'll tell him," Cowell said.

"He called my wife fat, too," Buddha exclaimed.

"Now listen," Cowell said, "them's obviously the words of a no-good drunk. Don't listen to drunks. Where would Stan be if he listened to drunks?" He slapped his hands onto Buddha's shoulders, massaged him like a boxer in a corner. "And let me tell you, if I see Angie in a halter top again, you're going to come up missing." He looked at Stan. "You mind watching my car while I drive Roy home?"

"I'll keep an eye out," Stan said. "Still working on that Falcon?"

"A blue Nova. Take a look. She'll be for sale soon."

Cowell returned to the parking lot. The front had passed and the rain fell with nothing more than occasional lightning and low rumbling thunder. He turned up his collar and threw away the cigarette. Roy's boots were sticking out of the driver's side backseat window. Water streamed off the heels. When Cowell opened the driver's door Roy jerked awake. The car smelled of booze; Cowell was thankful it didn't smell of anything else. Cowell reached over the front seat and tried, unsuccessfully, to pull Roy's feet inside by the wet cuffs of his jeans.

"Jesus," Cowell said with a grunt. "You're stiff as a corpse." He chopped Roy behind one knee, the way he broke the locking hinge when he folded up the legs on a card table. It worked. Roy dropped his foot against the armrest and, moaning, brought the other inside.

Cowell flicked rainwater onto Roy's face. "Do you need to pee or anything before we leave?" he said in a loud voice. "Roy? Goddamn. Last time I saw someone in your condition they'd been drinking what they cooked in the woods. Where're your keys?"

Roy's left hand crawled around the vicinity of his jacket pocket. Cowell found them, slid into the driver's seat, and started the car. He swore at the stubborn stick as they bobbed and hopped out of the lot. There was a flash of lightning, and without further preamble the rain came down in sheets. At least the wipers worked—he had helped replace them. The brakes inspired less confidence, and the muffler scraped the road at every bump. Still rigged with coat hangers, Cowell thought.

"What'd your landlady say?" he called back. Roy mumbled. Cowell asked again. On the third try Roy said she had missed the damaged floor.

A deep yawn caused Cowell to lose sight of the road for a moment. He turned the radio up loud, to stay alert and to share his suffering with Roy. He turned on the headlights. Raindrops streaked through the twin funnels of light like time-lapse photos of stars.

Searching the AM dial got him blasts of static, so Cowell ventured onto FM to occupy himself. The button on the left led to public radio, a hodgepodge of programs that, as far as Cowell could tell, operated free of logic or a schedule. Over the course of an evening they might offer the famous manifestos of history, recordings of hoboes banging on buckets, and angry women discussing of the decline of fiction—Cowell always imagined the women as bald, for some reason.

The second button took him to progressive underground rock. But he had quit listening to rock music after he emerged from the Navy and found the British shoveling dirt onto the Everly Brothers. Nothing at the other three buttons appealed to him, either.

Roy's hand appeared on the back of the seat. "Where we going?" he said.

"Where do you think we're going?" Cowell exclaimed. "To the Middle East to solve the oil crisis. I'm pleased to thank you for parking this piece of shit so it was visible from the road. You're a thoughtful son of a bitch. Where are we going? About ten feet on these bald tires.

"Look," he continued over his shoulder, "I'm not religious, so I don't know if God judges a man on the amount he drinks. But Phyllis does. Let me tell you something even crazier. She thinks you listen to me. 'Just about cars,' I tell her, but you know Phyl, she's got her ideas. And what're you doing going after Buddha? You've never been an angry drunk, as long as people don't poke at you. Leave him alone. It's bad enough his wife's being stuck more than a pincushion, and not by Buddha. Speaking of that, after tonight it'll be a hell of a long time before I see your sister's bare ass again. I don't need strains in my domestic situation, Roy. Jesus, look at the way we're pulling to the right. We're going to end up taking these mailboxes home with us."

Rain blurred the windshield as soon as the wipers passed. With an effort Cowell wrested the car onto the broken white line, to give them room in case they started to skid.

"More than anyone," he went on, calmer now, "a drinking man has to keep his car in good working order."

Roy tried to sound out Cowell's words. To the car's right a sign neared and whipped by—DO NOT PASS. The white glow of headlights rose behind the next hill and silhouetted Cowell's profile. Disconnected, as if watching a movie, Roy waited for the Ford to move off the white line. When it didn't, worry flared up inside him.

"You awake?" Cowell called. "Get sober in a hurry, because I can't carry you into the house."

Four headlights dawned atop the hill—bright and high off the road. Even as he closed his eyes against the glare Cowell jerked the wheel right and instinctively hit the brake. The back half of the Ford fishtailed into the oncoming lane. Cowell pumped the brakes and swung left. The bellow of the semi's horn sounded right outside his window. A wall of water smashed against the driver's side and Roy fell onto the seat, his arms raised against the wave. The wheel snapped back through Cowell's hands, swung the rear of the Ford right again. The back tires skidded through the gravel on the shoulder and dug into the turf beyond. There was a loud bang and a bump that nearly jolted Roy into the front seat—the rear tires had rolled over the muffler and spat it into the ditch.

The tires grabbed. With a jerk the back end reasserted itself, and the car came to a halt. They sat without moving until the radio static and the thunder brought them back.

"Shit-fire," Cowell gasped. "You in one piece?"

Roy made an affirmative noise.

Cowell flexed his hands—the skin on the inside of his fingers burned. "Bet you're sober now," he said. He turned to see the semi's hazards blinking. "Let me go tell this trucker he didn't kill us."

On the way Cowell paused at the scars they'd gouged in the grass and wildflowers, toed the exposed mud with his boot. Three feet of water—every bit of it—had collected in the ditch. He slicked back his hair and jogged to meet the truck driver. By the time he got back he felt steady enough to light one of Roy's cigarettes. He shuddered, from his wet clothes or an aftershock from the near miss. In the rearview mirror he could see Roy lying back, his head lolling atop the seat.

Cowell and Phyl dumped Roy onto the bed, wet boots and all. When they were gone, Cammy and Grub dragged their pillows and blankets and stuffed animals to Eric's room. Eric helped them make a bed, one blanket spread on the floor and one over each of them. At Grub's request he tiptoed to the girls' room and retrieved their night-light.

"Turn off the radio," Cammy demanded.

Aunt Phyl said you should make accommodations for guests. While he thought her far enough down the road to disobey, he knew from experience that Cammy was willing to wake up their father to complain regardless of the state he was in. Once, back when Roy worked nights, she woke him up several hours too early because Eric refused to let her watch the test pattern station on TV. Another time he passed out after an evening at the bars, and Cammy shook him awake because Eric made her stop drumming on the pots and pans. These were the acts of a crazy person, as far as Eric was concerned. But you had to take the threat seriously.

He turned off the radio. "I'm going to get a drink of water," he whispered.

"Don't wake him up," Cammy said.

Eric sighed at the irony.

When he went downstairs the next morning the odor of egg water mixed with mountain-grown coffee filled the house. His father said hello, and Eric answered, and that was it. During a break in the cartoons Eric went for more milk and glimpsed Roy out in the driveway on one knee alongside the Ford. He seemed to be gliding his hand over the left rear tire.

ONCE, WHEN HE WAS ELEVEN, Roy had watched two of his cousins steal several cases of Coca-Cola from a parked delivery truck. More cases than they could carry very far, in fact. When Dombey held out the coins, Roy thought about how strange it was that a fortune could fit inside a jangling plastic bag that weighed about as much as the two cans of pop he had seen from his cousins' heist.

"A third," Dombey said as he handed over the bag. "What changed your mind?"

"I never made up my mind," Roy said.

"Okay, smart-ass, what made up your mind?"

"Shit comes up."

Dombey laughed. "It do indeed. One week, and I'll get the stuff from you."

"You're sure?"

"The deal's halfway closed already. We wouldn't have touched the shit otherwise. What would we do with it? I don't have extensive underworld contacts. And my brother-in-law's so dumb he'd put that Roman coin in a pop machine. Don't sweat it. A week from now, we'll be having a nice quiet beer at Stan's. We'll buy a pitcher, surprise the hell out of him."

Roy kept the coins under his seat on the drive home. Once on the road he felt jittery. He tapped the steering wheel, let out deep breaths, tried to ignore what felt like a live wire snaking around his insides. Nothing unexpected, he told himself. It was an unusual situation. He'd get used to it and probably forget the coins. A convenience store sign appeared on the right. Milk and bread, he thought. But he passed. He didn't want to push it. How many stories had he read where a crook was caught in some arrogant, dumb-shit move like wearing a dead guy's stolen watch or trying to burn state's evidence in a backyard barbeque? Roy eased his foot off the gas, slowed down to the speed limit. A cop car, he noticed, was parked in the convenience store lot.

That's a sign, he said to himself.

A weight lifted as Roy turned into the driveway. At the house he found the girls watching TV and Eric in his bedroom banging on a tin can. He chased Eric downstairs. Roy removed the coins from the pocket of his jacket. Another deep sigh. Without realizing it he glanced out the window, down the driveway. First he hid the coins in his dresser drawer. Too obvious, he thought. He considered under the mattress, but Phyl might find it while changing the sheets. He considered the basement, but he could not always account for the kids—at least they knew to stay out of his room. He even considered too-clever detective novel tricks like dangling the bag at the end of a cord out the window. In the end he tucked it into a nook on his closet shelf, between a shoebox of photos and a small green vinyl handbag that had belonged to Jean.

On his way out of the bedroom, Roy looked out the window again. As he turned to go, he started at the Grub standing in the doorway, blinking, her diaper at her knees, and he was so startled it was all he could do to not cry out.

THE CABBIE TURNED and said, "Harper Elementary School."
"Pull over here."

Deb jogged up the front steps, one hand on the rail, the other under her belly, supporting the baby. A towheaded crossing guard held the door for her. No sooner had she spotted the front office than Maria Spinoza appeared in the door. She wore an un-fashionable brown blouse with black slacks that failed to slim a pair of so-called child-bearing hips. Deb hated that term, but all the same she knew that in three months she would envy those hips. When Maria grinned, Deb saw the tiny wrinkle, a sort of second smile, that always appeared above her lip. Maria gestured at Deb's stomach and bent over to embrace her.

"We have pills to prevent this sort of thing," Maria said.

As they broke, Deb said, "Well, you marry a younger man . . ."

"Come on back," Maria said. "I cleared files off a chair in anticipation of your visit."

Maria led her to a small corner office. It reminded Deb of a private detective's lair, the fan in the window and parallel lines of sunlight sketched by the blinds onto one wall. The generous dark woodwork and cream-colored walls complimented one another. The cherrywood desk was worthy of a crooked alderman. Out of necessity Maria had stacked ugly metal storage shelves with manila folders and office supplies.

Maria motioned Deb to a chair and sat on the corner of the desk, one leg over the other. "It's embarrassing when the children are neater than you are. Since we caught up on personal biz over the phone, and since you're wearing a ball-breaker ensemble, can I assume you're here to enroll your new arrival? I warn you, we usually advise parents to hold off until the kids are teething."

"It's my sister's son," Deb began.

"The one you mentioned on the phone?" Maria said.

"Yes. What's the deadline for enrolling a student for the fall term?"

Maria hesitated and used the pause to study Deb with the interrogating eye she used to break underachievers and truants. Deb, however, knew to wait her out. They had become friends when Deb's daughter attended Harper—Maria the just-promoted administrator, Deb the involved young parent to end all involved young parents. Whatever Maria's ambitions—be they grants, new equipment, or a field trip to the symphony—Deb enlisted, from doing research to wrangling students. More than once they had formed an alliance to get Emma to study the subjects she dismissed with such 90th-percentile words as *dismal* and *interminable*. Em's middle school grades testified to the effectiveness of such attention. That Maria managed it by channeling the stubbornness instead of breaking it awed Deb, though on occasion she had pled for the other method.

"It's this Friday," Maria answered. "But just between us, it's not firm."

"I won't pretend Eric's going to graduate med school in his teens," Deb said, "but he's bright and he's motivated."

Deb went into her spiel. She played up Eric's time at Akhmatova and played down his home life, and did not believe for a second that she managed to allay Maria's usual list of questions on the latter. From there she bounced to the meeting with Miss Birch and added her own observations on his dedication. "No one knows where this astronomy obsession comes from," Deb ended.

"Kids go through phases," Maria said.

"Unless he's in an environment that provides a chance for him to explore this interest, it'll never be more than a phase," Deb replied. "You agree there are children who pursue a life path they discover at a young age? I don't mean Mozart. Just accomplished practitioners in the arts, science, even business."

"I'm sure Howard Hughes ran a successful lemonade stand," Maria said. "The tuition hasn't gone down, Deb."

"He would qualify for a hardship grant."

Maria sat forward, sounded even more sympathetic than she looked. "You know the politics and you know who decides. A lot of the kids we choose have only one parent. Or one grandparent. Or an older sibling who works three jobs. I'm not saying you couldn't make a case for Eric, certainly not after the work you've put into the school, but it'll raise a ruckus. Why not Akhmatova?"

"His father can't handle the logistics," Deb said. "If Eric lived in the city, I could get him here."

Maria picked up a legal pad, clicked the end of a pen. "Tell me about his home life."

"Well, there's Jean."

"Besides that."

"It's alcohol, mainly." Deb felt frustration welling up, tried to stop it and the tag-along rise of her temper. "But that isn't the real problem," she said. "There's a psychological component. It would still exist even if he quit drinking tomorrow. I don't know how to put this except to say he's teaching his children to lose."

"Lose," Maria said.

"To live with low expectations—with no expectations. Jean wasn't that way. She pushed. She tried to be more. Maybe Roy wants more, but he isn't capable and he never has been."

"Because of the drinking."

"Because he's weak," Deb said. "Roy is about the here and now. The future, as a concept, is unfathomable to him."

"That all his energy goes to present-day survival is understandable," Maria replied. "Under the circumstances."

"No," Deb said, and she rapped the arm of the chair. "It was always this way, Mo. It's how he deals with the world, and it permeates that house, permeates every cell in those kids. He survives. That's all. And what does studying astronomy have to do with survival? It's a pointless use of energy in strictly Darwinian terms. In the world where Eric lives, learning astronomy is about as practical as learning to herd camels. No one can conceive it could ever matter, Roy least of all."

Maria meandered to the window, pretended to be distracted by the street scene outside.

"How do we explain that in terms the Board will understand?" she mused.

"What I've described is as significant as any other problem with a home environment," Deb said.

"I agree. But the Board usually makes its judgments based on sociology, not psychology."

Deb removed her glasses and rubbed her eyes. Did this have to be an ordeal? Could the school not reward her ten thousand hours of free labor?

Don't think that way, she thought. That was for Emma, and you got a good return on the investment. She blinked at her tears.

"Do you want some water?" Maria murmured.

"Please."

Maria stepped out. Deb went to the window. Her deep exhalations—her defense against more tears—swirled the dust motes in the narrow beams of sunlight that came through the blinds. When Maria came back, Deb returned to her chair and Maria to the corner of the desk.

"You've mentioned Harper to the father?" she said.

"I wanted to make sure it was possible," Deb said. "To lend weight to my argument."

"How about to your daughter and husband?"

Deb took a drink of water. "First things first."

"Oh, Deb," Maria sighed.

"Is it possible?"

"With God and you all things are possible. Do we need to rehearse the Board's counter-arguments? That he'd be taking the place of someone else, et cetera?"

"Every child here takes the place of someone else," Deb replied.

"I didn't think that would work."

Deb tried to smile. "With a pregnant woman? A lioness defending the young?"

"That's some real Darwin," Maria said. "As you know, there are people I have to speak with to get the process rolling. Once that happens we can brainstorm an approach to the Board. I'm sticking my neck out, Deb. I have to know you're not just testing the waters."

"I'm serious."

"Is this possible for you? With the baby?"

"Yes."

Maria scribbled something on her calendar. "I'll get you an ap packet right now. I have one condition. Talk to Fergus." To Deb's glare she added, "This is for the good of the child and the good of the school."

It took Deb a moment to rein in. "All right."

"Call me when the packet's done." Maria finished writing on the legal pad. "I have to keep a certain amount of distance. But provide the razzle dazzle, and I'll help with the necessary subtle touches."

They embraced with the packet between them. Tears threatened again once Deb was outside. She rushed across the street against the yellow light and later imagined her pregnant waddle was the reason the cars, inexplicably, did not honk at her. She hurried into the park—trying to stuff the packet into her briefcase, fumbling with her sunglasses—and finally, sweating and winded, settled onto an empty bench. Letting her arm dangle off the end of the bench, she leaned over and picked a few blades of grass, rolled them between her thumb and forefinger. The grass's texture reminded her of straw, and that reminded her of an incident from the previous autumn, after Jean's death.

A crying Eric had come flying into the dining room. Unable to get anything coherent out of him, she'd followed him to the side of the house. For whatever reason Eric had been allowed to fall into an alliance with the Garland brothers. During the morning the threesome had pursued a rat around the buildings until cornering it in a shallow crawl space in the foundation of a nearby lab. The Garlands, indulged by their parents in all the nonlethal weaponry of childhood, had taken aim with glorified slingshots—Eric called them wrist rockets. When the metal bullets ran out, they used bits of gravel.

The rat had staggered from the crawl space during a lull. One floppy ear was bent over its face. Bright red blood covered the haunch, the neck, and the puff of white fur that had been a tail. A piece of straw stuck out of one ruined eye like an arrow.

It was not a rat, but a rabbit. The animal had shivered as Deb approached. The Garlands huddled a safe distance away, both fascinated and ready to run. Deb held the rabbit against her body. When she passed Eric, she shouted for him to look at her and she jerked the animal so close to his face he screamed, and she glared down at him until he blurred, and she wondered aloud how he of all people could wish death on something.

The house had been empty. Roy and the girls were off on some errand. Deb put the rabbit on the dining room table and surrounded it with her arms and wept.

She wept more quietly now.

In time the sun moved around her shade tree. The heat of it on her black suit convinced her to leave. She walked home. Gathering storm clouds blocked the sun just as she turned down her street. It was easy to predict what Fergus might say. "You're one of those people who needs to keep a florist on retainer." "Maybe you should've married Gandhi." Something clever.

She paused on the front steps to listen to the clatter of his typewriter. It would be necessary to interrupt his work. Otherwise the discussion might bleed into dinnertime and be overheard by Emma, and it was too early to invite that set of strong opinions. Later, she would call Maria and apologize. A humbling evening, in other words. But all things were possible with God and Deborah Frank, she thought. Even saying "I need." Even saying "I'm sorry."

AFTER SATURDAY PRACTICES, Coach Garland hung around to talk with parents and coaches. That left Eric with time to fill before he was taken home. He crossed the street to Nathan Jail and bounced a baseball against the wall to practice catching high flies.

Dirt covered his back and behind. Johnny Garland, continuing a team tradition, plowed over all of the smaller players manning second base during the stolen-base drill. Eric, holding his glove shut with his bare hand, was sent flying three times, as was the ball. He had, however, hit the ball twice during batting practice. Both hits landed behind first base near the end of the bleachers. "Little late on your swing," Coach Garland said. On the next pitch Eric let her rip before the ball was halfway to home plate. That got a good laugh. Still, two fouls.

Mrs. Garland picked up her boys—Eric remembered his mom used to say they were being taken back into custody—but Julie remained. She dug her father's glove out of the equipment bag and joined Eric at the wall. Without asking she brushed off his back and behind.

"You look like Pig-Pen," she exclaimed, waving away the dust.

"I wouldn't if your stupid brother didn't knock me down."

Julie wriggled her hand into the glove. "Will you throw me some?"

"You can throw if you want," Eric said.

"You make it do better pop-ups."

So Eric did the throwing. Through experimentation he had learned that standing closer to the wall allowed him to throw at a steeper angle. That in turn caused the ball to pop higher in the air. He watched in admiration as Julie chased down every throw. She whipped her limbs in all directions, contorting her body for her crazy jumps, heedless of tumbling on the cement, spinning to throw the ball back to him and holding her pose until he caught it, when he caught it.

"I'm better than you," she said.

"I know," he groaned.

"You got two good hits, though."

That thrilled him, but he said, "They were fouls."

"Everyone hits fouls. Stop throwing. I'm sweating." She walked forward, dropped the ball in his glove. "Joel says you're a know-it-all about astrology."

"It's astronomy," Eric said. "No, I'm not. Joel's a know-it-all. He thinks he knows everything about sports."

"Emily Kruger said she wishes you'd go back to your old school."

Feeling his cheeks burning, Eric turned and tossed the ball. It came back as a grounder. "At least I don't throw up at school every week."

"That's not her fault."

"It's not my fault I'm at this cruddy school, either."

"She's got a nervous stomach," Julie said. "Do you know what Michelle says about you?"

"Why are you telling me these mean things?" Eric exclaimed. "Shut up. I don't care what stupid Michelle McCabe says. She can't even tie her shoes." He tried to continue and then, sputtering in frustration, he flung his glove at her. Like most of his throws it sailed well over the target. Julie watched it fly past.

As he stomped after the glove she said, "You don't have to get so pissed off. Michelle didn't say anything bad."

Eric scooped up the glove and continued across the playground, swatting at the chains on the swing set as he passed. For a moment Julie tried to call him back. As she caught up to him she took his shirt. Eric spun and smacked her across the bare arm with his glove. She stepped back, shocked, her hand going to the welt on her forearm. To Eric's enormous surprise it looked like she might cry. Then she threw down her glove and with a scream tackled Eric into the sandbox.

They wrestled for a full minute. Most of the time Eric stayed dug in and kept his eyes closed against the sand and her wind-whipped hair. A piercing whistle interrupted her attempts to roll him on his back.

"Let's go," Coach Garland called.

Julie slapped Eric in the shoulder as she stood up. "You didn't have to hit me. Look at the mark on my arm."

Eric could not answer. He was wiping sand from his tongue onto his shirt.

Coach Garland pronounced them unfit to sit in the cab of his truck. Once they were in the bed he leaned out the window. "No standing up back there," he barked. "You understand me?"

"Yes," both said. "Go fast over the hills," Julie added.

Eric watched the fields go by. The neat rows of seedlings seemed to emanate from the same point, like spokes on an immense wheel. Julie crawled halfway through the window of the cab to ask a question. She emerged and sat again. For about twenty seconds. First she fiddled with the equipment bag's drawstring. Then she removed one of the bruised baseballs and with exaggerated care set it in a groove on the bed of the truck. It began to bounce. For every up a down. Gravity, Eric thought. The sound of the ball rolling brought a cry from Mr. Garland. Julie retrieved it, sat back next to Eric, held it at arm's length.

"If you look through one eye," she called, "the ball blocks the sun, because it's a circle."

Roy was bent over the Ford's engine when the Garland pickup arrived at the house. Julie called a hello, and her father waved from the cab as Eric hopped out of the bed. Then the pickup tore away, kicking up gravel and dust. Julie gave a shriek of pleasure.

"How was practice?" Roy asked.

Eric shrugged and headed for the porch.

"Hold on," Roy said.

"I have to do something," Eric said.

"Come here a second, damn it." As Eric approached the car, Roy drained his Olympia and used it to gesture. "How'd you get so dirty?"

"Julie tackled me in the sandbox," Eric said. "We were wrestling."

"It looks like you lost." He shook the beer can. The tab rattled inside. "Do me a favor and throw this out."

"Do you want another one?" Eric asked.

"Not right now."

Eric turned to go.

"Hold on, hold on," Roy said. "You never answered my question."

"I said I got dirty in the sandbox."

"How was practice?"

"Fine."

A dozen other questions rose in Roy's mind. Do you like baseball any better? Does the hitting or the fielding seem any easier? Might Coach Garland put him in the infield once in a while? The words tumbled around his mouth, but he said nothing. What kept him from asking? Why not take the kid in his arms and promise him he'd be as good as any other player on the team? What kept him from doing that?

Eric seemed anxious to go inside.

"You want to play catch later?" Roy said.

"Okay."

"Take your clothes off on the porch."

Eric usually protested, out of modesty and because Phyl had passed along some superstition about entering a house the same way you left it. But today he stripped down to his underwear, shook out the pants, and left the heap behind him.

Not long afterward, Roy gave in to distraction and returned to the house. A pink plastic ball sat in the center of the dining room table. Eric, still in his underwear, knelt at eye level to it. With great deliberateness he rolled a baseball from left to right. As it passed between his face and the tennis ball he stopped, inched it toward him a bit more, and paused. Roy watched without a sound. So did Grub and the dog.

"Can I help?" Roy finally said.

"No," Eric replied. "I understand now."

ROY AND DOMBEY PULLED the park's sole picnic table to the edge of the parking lot while the rest of the crew gathered for lunch. Fraser popped the trunk and turned on the radio. Tiny, the foreman, arrived from the other direction bearing a plate covered with a checkered towel. He pulled it off with the flair of a Vegas magician. The crew cheered.

"Double strawberry ripple cake," he said. "Courtesy of a catering job that cancelled on my wife last night. Pass it around. I didn't want to share, but Shari insisted."

Dombey took a piece of cake, passed the plate to Roy. "This here's the next best thing to pussy," he said.

"You're in a good mood today," Tiny said. "Finally find some girl who'd listen to your sweet talk?"

"Got high energy, is all." He winked at Roy. "Beat the Burlington Northern on the way in. Best way to wake up."

"You should try coffee," Tiny said.

"It hurts my stomach."

Bramm approached, lunch bucket in hand. They all dreaded his report of last night's fishing. In the course of working with him, Roy had learned enough about northern pike to qualify for the Fish and Wildlife Service.

"Catfish were biting last night," Bramm began.

Dombey caught Roy's eye.

"Did you hear India's got The Bomb?" Dombey said.

Through his tuna sandwich Tiny said, "When did India get The Bomb?"

"Sometime before they exploded it yesterday."

"Can I talk about my catfish?" Bramm said.

"Not until we sort this out," Dombey replied.

"Okay, so who says India has The Bomb?"

"I don't know, man. The news."

Roy wiped his mouth. "Good cake, Tiny."

"Shari's doing the Lord's work," Tiny said.

Fraser grunted in approval. He wore a very large wooden cross, had nine kids.

"Who would be stupid enough to give India an atomic bomb?" Bramm exclaimed.

"Don't know," Dombey said.

"They developed it," Roy said.

"No way," Bramm said, shaking his head.

"Why not?"

"Because cobras kill thousands of people there every year. You're telling me these people can't stop snakes but they built a nuclear weapon?"

"They got killer fish, too," Dombey said. "Big ol' perch jump out of the rivers, take them tiny Indian guys at the throat, chomp. It's worse than piranhas."

A station wagon pulled up. Tiny went to the driver's side window of Fraser's car, leaned in, and turned down the radio. Gordon was of Lebanese heritage, wore sunglasses, a short-sleeved shirt with a necktie, and an enormous key ring. Roy had worked for and socialized with him for years. Their wives had been good friends, and Eric got along with his sons.

"Pack it up," Gordon said, miming a lifting motion. "The sonofabitch's check bounced again. Up, up! Go home."

"Do we get paid for the day?" Dombey asked.

"What do you think?" Gordon exclaimed, his forehead veins bulging.

"What about tomorrow?" Tiny said.

"I don't know about tomorrow. If he doesn't find the cash, I don't know. You show up at the Cherry Creek site in the morning." Turning to the others, he said, "The rest of you, I'll call if this guy comes through."

"I don't need a day off," Dombey said.

"Don't worry, he'll scrape it together in the next day or two. He's screwed around so long he's running out of time on the permit."

All of them began to pack up. Roy caught Dombey's eye, and the two of them hung back just long enough for Fraser to walk out of earshot. Their cars were parked next to one another. Walking together looked natural. Before Roy could say anything, Dombey told him the deal might wrap up by the weekend. He had a good feeling.

Roy drove off the site calculating the money lost by going home early. The only good side was the possibility they'd see future overtime to meet the permit's deadline. Those Saturdays looked a long ways away, though.

He pulled into a corner store. One day Dombey had chatted up the midday man, learned the guy had spent several years as a freak-in-residence at a California university while earning his Master's. A personal crisis—the guy refused to give details— convinced him to trade his old bicycle and simplicity for what he referred to as The Life as It Exists.

The midday man gave Roy the Boy Scout salute. Though Roy told himself he was only buying cigarettes, he stopped in front of the pay phone. Midafternoon, midweek. She might be home. If her husband was, too, well, then it became an hour or two of socializing with adults before he went home to greet the kids. Roy glanced toward the counter. But very little that happened in the store interested the guy.

She answered after two rings.

"Hi, Lori," he said, then he cleared his throat. "It's Roy Conlon."

"Royyyy," she said sleepily. "Ahoy, Roy."

"How's it going?"

"Fair to partly cloudy," she said. "Doing some housework, listening to music. When are we going to see you again?"

Roy let out his breath. A fastball down the middle.

"Actually," he said, "we've been cut loose for the afternoon—"

"What a lucky day."

"Yeah." He took a breath. "I wondered if you guys were around."

"Around? Sure. Here, there, and everywhere. Do you have the kids with you?"

"I'm coming from work," Roy said.

"Right," she said. "It's Wednesday."

A long pause.

"Maybe you're busy," Roy said.

The hippy-dippy voice vanished. "Come over."

"Should I bring anything?"

Another pause. "Edward's not here."

The midday man rang up a few candy bars along with the cigarettes.

For a year before Grub's birth, and for several months after, Roy and his family lived in an apartment across the hall from Lori and her husband, Edward. In those days Lori was a grad student in an on-again, off-again relationship with her thesis. Edward, a more serious student and much more serious stoner, had risen into the higher consciousness of a PhD program. Roy liked him. Edward was aware that philosophy boggled the layman and so held no illusions that Big Questions played any role in the lives of everyday people trying to pay rent or keep their kids out of traffic. Thus, philosophy only intruded on his conversations when he'd gone too far into the prodigious reserve of grass the couple kept stored in the baby coffin in their bedroom.

Roy drove by the building twice before parking a few blocks up the street. A Helping Hand sign remained in one of the ground-level windows; the nine in the address above the door was still missing. Roy walked around to look at the back. The parking lot was a pond of asphalt indifferently poured into a circle and now sprouting weeds and scrawny wildflowers. A field separated the lot from a chemical factory.

Roy climbed the same narrow stairs with the same mustard-toned carpet to the same door with the same peace sign sticker under the eyehole. When Lori opened the door her stick-figure body was covered with a short silk robe bought during a trip to Japan. She'd pushed her stringy dishwater blond hair behind her ears.

"Come in," she said.

He did so.

Lori gestured to the kitchen. "Do you want a drink? Coffee? Tea? A stiff belt, as my dad says?"

Though he found it hard to breathe, Roy managed to say, "Only if you do."

"Not particularly." Now she gestured through the living room. "Should we go or—?"

Roy nodded.

"It's nice to see you," Lori said. She rubbed his hands, one after the other. The last time they were together, she had said she adored his rough hands.

AFTER, LORI EASED OFF OF HIM and fell back onto the pile of tumbled sheets. Sweat had turned the hair at her temples a dark brown. Roy peeled his back off the sheet and sat on the edge of the bed to catch his breath.

"Be right back," Lori said. While she was gone Roy rearranged the candy bars on the night table and, as the delay stretched further, paged through *Erica Wilson's Embroidery Book*. Lori vaulted onto the bed, kissed each of his shoulders. Roy, uncomfortable, just slightly wriggled to free himself from her grip and reached for the night table.

"I brought you a few candy bars," he said. "If you still eat them."

"Perfect," Lori said.

"You know, we have this book at home."

"I gave it to Jean," Lori exclaimed. "For Christmas. You don't remember? Don't tell me you don't remember. For the next five months we could hear her swearing because she could never get it right."

"She wasn't much of a homemaker," Roy said, putting the book back.

Lori clenched her ankles and rocked back, laughing. "My favorite was the time she threw out the entire batch of fudge still in the pan. I'll never forget it. Eric dug it out of the garbage can. He and Cammy had chocolate all over them. Of course I had no trouble joining them. I swear I miss her volcanic temper more than anything."

Roy did not reply.

"Should I not bring her up?" Lori said.

"It's not that."

Lori tied her hair back, vaulted off the bed and pulled on her robe. "Guilt is not necessary," she said. "In the past year Edward has pruned his life of everything except Martin Heidegger and Maui Wowie. Or maybe it's about Jean?"

"No," Roy said.

"Don't get hung up on Edward. If he walked in right now he wouldn't even care. He wouldn't even notice. Come on. I'll make tea."

Lori neglected to tie her robe closed. That she was using the stove was the only reason she wore anything at all. Roy preferred to dress. When he rejoined her a teapot was on the stove and two cups on the table, one with the sticks-and-leaves mixture concocted for her by a Taiwanese refugee near campus, the other a bag of Lipton for Roy. She apologized for having no iced tea on hand. Roy, watching her move around, tried to dredge up some emotion. Not love—he wasn't ridiculous—but at least a little affection. Anything seemed better than just after-sex drowsiness.

"How's my goddaughter?" Lori said. "Still fat?"

"Grub's as skinny as a frog now," he answered.

"Any sign of the problems you have with Cammy?"

"It doesn't look like it. She's better coordinated. Eric teaches her new words. Astronomy terms. He's into astronomy now."

Lori poured water into the cup in front of him. "He gave up *Speed Racer*? I didn't think anything short of a Maoist reeducation camp could distract him from that show. An astronomy bag, though? How did that happen?"

"Beats the shit out of me," Roy sighed.

"I think I have a good picture of him around here somewhere." After a moment she returned with two framed photos. "Make that pictures," she said.

The first Roy remembered clearly. Two or three years earlier Eric had contracted impetigo. The doctor painted his face with a purplish solution to cure it. Edward and a lot of other people teased him about it, circus and clown jokes and the like. Fortunately it took only a couple of applications to clear things up. The second picture showed Eric holding a fire safety certificate. Bright sunlight had turned his hair red. To look at him on that day was to see only Jean in the hair and freckles and the gangly posture afforded by long limbs. Roy saw no visible signs of himself.

Roy told Lori about the tin-can planetarium, the nights with the telescope, the dining room table experiment on the movement of celestial bodies. "His teacher wants me to encourage him," he concluded. "But he works on this shit all the time. I'd like him to leave his room once in a while."

Over the top of her cup she said, "Maybe it's a comfort thing."

Roy shrugged, but he felt uneasy. For one thing he found Lori's intense attention disconcerting. Never mind that she knew, even loved, his son. Considering the situation, the last thing Roy wanted was an in-depth discussion about his family. He was sorry he had brought up Eric at all.

"You know what they say," Lori went on, pointing at the ceiling. "The final frontier. Someone's going to have to know his way around up there. Except he'd have to join the military first. That would be a drag for a sensitive kid." She pointed into her tea. "I see from the message at the bottom of the cup that this isn't your main worry."

"I'm just wondering where he got it, that's all."

"You don't see yourself in him, right?"

That caught Roy by surprise. Lori took advantage of the pause to light one of the roaches piled in a FABULOUS LAS VEGAS ashtray.

"Puff?" she said.

"No, thanks," Roy replied.

After drawing in what remained she sat back, put one bare foot up on the table. "When it comes to parenting advice, I can't speak from experience. I spent some time around itty-bitty Eric, though. Wherever astronomy and all the rest comes from, it belongs to him now. That's not a knock on you. Look at my father. Former Navy admiral, football star in college. Graduated with honors from the U.S. Naval Academy and at one point in his life turned down a chance to go to the Sorbonne. Do I look like the daughter of that résumé? Something along the way possesses us. Either Eric goes with it, or he gets a permanent inner conflict where what you forced on him butts up against what he's being urged to do by the Fantastic Total Him."

"Psychological bullshit," Roy said with a sigh.

"The Oedipus complex is psychological bullshit," Lori exclaimed. "I'm telling you the truth. Denying what you are takes a lot of energy away from living."

"I'm not saying I'm opposed to astronomy or anything else," Roy replied. He jiggled the ashtray. "This must be some potent shit."

"What I'm telling you is potent shit."

Roy had the sudden urge to tell her about the coins. Are you nuts? he wondered. What could she do? Tell you it's all right? Shit, more likely it'd change her opinion of you. But the temptation was, for a moment, overwhelming. As a rule Roy did not indulge in self-examination, but the urge was powerful enough to lead him to ask why he would risk her good opinion or even involve her in a crime.

Lori's voice broke into his thoughts. "Are you okay?"

"Why?" he asked.

"The look on your face. Are you still worried about Edward?"

"It's a money thing. Unrelated."

Raising her eyebrows, she said, "I'm glad I could take your mind off of it. Can I bum a legal smoke?"

He slid his new pack across to her. "I should go."

"When will you visit again?" she said.

"It's hard to find time."

"I don't care about the time," Lori said, "as long as this isn't the last time." She gave a yawn. "That's not bad—it's rhetorically daring to rhyme a word with the same word."

MISS BIRCH HAD ASSIGNED each student in the class a report on his or her hobby. Five kids went each day, and one of the Tuesday presentations fell to Eric. The afternoon before, he arrived home and, after a snack, began to select which of the cans to take with him. When he had decided on a half-dozen examples he looked for something to carry them in. The box wouldn't work. People on the bus would grab stuff from inside it and, anyway, the bottom was about to break. But there was nothing better in his room, the guest room, or the basement except, maybe, a red suitcase, his mother's, but it stood two-thirds as tall as he did. As he stood looking at it he remembered she had a small, green handbag.

Roy had never forbidden his children to enter his room. As far as he knew, however, they understood not to do so. Eric mostly obeyed the unexpressed order, only went in during sprawling adventures with his Hot Wheels cars or when for some reason he wanted to look out of the room's north-facing window. It occurred to him to ask Aunt Phyl to get the handbag off the closet shelf, but at the moment she was busy cooking supper.

The tallest upstairs chair had wheels, and Eric pushed it in from the guest bedroom as quietly as possible. When it was in place before the open closet he returned to the top of the staircase to see if Phyl called up. But she hadn't heard. He guided the chair to underneath the handbag, climbed up, and steadied himself with a hand on the jamb. As he rose onto tiptoes he felt the wheels move a fraction. He froze. They stopped. With a deep breath he reached and got his fingertips on the handbag. But he had to lean and that moved the wheels again. Quickly Eric felt for a hold. Just as the chair threatened to move under him he jerked his hand back. The handbag came off with it. So did an old alarm clock and a jangling plastic bag. Afraid, he grabbed the jamb. It saved him, but the handbag bounced off the side of the closet and the clothes hanging inside before landing with a bang, while the plastic bag flew past his hip and burst open on the floor.

Coins of many kinds bounced and rolled in all directions. One disappeared under the bed. Another traveled in a wide arc toward the heat duct in the corner and Eric, hand over his mouth, watched it bump across the floor—and miss the grill before coming to a stop against the floorboard.

"Eric?" Phyl called.

Eric eased down and then stood in place for a few seconds.

"Eric? Did your cans fall?"

"I'm picking up," he said.

The coins reflected the overhead light, and for an instant the shapes he saw mesmerized him. Then terror returned. As fast and as quietly as he could he pushed one of the strays into the pile around the bag. As he did he noticed its strangeness. Age had worn off some of the details; its size and weight and color and the letters on it differed from what he had seen on any other coin. But Eric only studied it a second.

He had just emerged with a Liberty Dollar from under the bed when he heard the footsteps on the stairs. His father had returned home.

Roy's shock at the sight of the coins was complete, not heartstopping but time-stopping. For about three seconds. He descended on Eric, pulled him off the floor by the wrist and ankle, let go of the latter so that Eric swung wildly, helpless, and again and again Roy brought his open hand down. The first blows fell in shocked silence. Fear and pain then caused Eric to wail as he dangled in the air like a caught fish, flailing with his free arm to block the blows, blows that fell until the friction of Roy's hand against his son's corduroys caused his palm to burn.

Roy dropped him and shouted in a voice as big as the world, "What were you doing in the fucking closet?"

There was no answer through Eric's screams. For a moment Roy fought down an urge to start in on him again. But his fear returned at the sight of the coins. They had scattered everywhere. He realized he had no idea as to the number of coins, or what kind Dombey had stolen. In fact, he had not so much as looked inside the bag since the moment it was dropped into his hand.

Roy was up past midnight searching. Twice he pronounced himself satisfied but, unable to relax, started again. Worry drove him out of bed a third time.

The next morning he started his day under the bed and in the corners of the room. Finally going downstairs, he prepared breakfast for the girls. Eric did not appear. From the bottom of the stairs he heard the familiar rattle of cans. He called Eric's name. Again. No answer. "Eric, don't make me come up there," he warned, before he felt ridiculous for saying it. When Eric still ignored him, the anger from the previous night welled up again. Roy climbed the stairs.

Eric sat cross-legged in front of his pile of cans.

"Come down and eat," Roy said.

"I'm not hungry," Eric replied.

"I said get downstairs."

"I have to finish with this can so I can take it to school for my project."

Roy drew a breath. "I'm not telling you again."

"It's for school—"

A sweep of Roy's boot scattered the cans against the far wall.

"Goddamn it," he barked, "get downstairs, now."

To his relief—or so Roy thought, since he could not admit to his feeling of satisfaction—Eric stood. But that was all he did, stood and stared down at his violated work space, fists balled, tears on his cheeks, sniffling as he breathed.

"Eric," Roy said.

Eric's fists tightened, and his jaw. "I have to. For school." And he looked up with anger and betrayal in his eyes, familiar anger and familiar betrayal, the image of his mother, her son, *hers* and no other, with the set of her bones shaping his face, and the straight line of the mouth, and the way he lowered his chin to glare from the tops of his eye sockets.

"Look," Roy said, "you can take the handbag."

"I don't want it."

Jean again.

"Don't be an asshole."

Eric did not move.

"Son," Roy said, "it's very important you keep those coins a secret. Look at me. Do you understand? They're a gift. A present. But it's a surprise. You can't tell anyone at school or Aunt Phyl. Don't even say there is a present or a secret. All right? It'll ruin the surprise. Eric?"

"All right."

"I'm not kidding."

"All right."

But all day Roy heard Eric's voice telling Julie Garland or Phyl, or another classmate, or Cowell. Cowell who volunteered with the sheriff's department. A thousand times he asked himself: Why had the damned kid chosen that day to dig in the closet? Why did I put the coins where they could fall? Did I miss one? Roy left work at a jog. On the drive home he came close to racing a freight at the crossing. By the time it passed he had lit his third cigarette and the inside of the car looked like a foggy morning. At home he began to look around the bedroom again before, out of frustration with the search and his fear, he made himself stop. A little while later, as he stood in the dining room estimating the size of the floor he had to replace, a flash of light off a windshield caused his heart to jump. But it was only Garland bringing Eric home from practice.

EVERY SPRING, AUNT PHYL PILED late Christmas presents and a pair of suitcases into the station wagon and drove to Missouri to see their older sister, who lived on a farm halfway between New Madrid and the Arkansas state line. Parts of the family land remained buckled from the 1811 earthquake that had rerouted the Mississippi River. Roy had forgotten about her trip until Thursday evening when Phyl, cutting up chicken for dinner, reminded him. He held in a groan.

"Your sister-in-law's willing to pitch in," Phyl said, still sawing at the bird. She avoided using Deborah's name, as if the woman might appear in a flash of fire and brimstone.

"How do you know?" Roy said.

"I called her." A thigh snapped off. "Cammy gave me the number."

That must've been a surprise at the other end, Roy thought.

"She's fixing to start her maternity leave," Phyl continued. "Looking after your kids will keep her strong. It's not like she's been ordered to stay in bed."

"Hey, if she's willing, great."

Phyl began to stack the pieces of chicken. "Going to storm," she said. "I hope that baseball coach doesn't get those little guys struck by lightning. He'd play through a tornado."

The April tornadoes in Xenia, Ohio, had had a tremendous effect on Phyl. For several days she broke her own injunction against the news and watched as much of it as she could get, even drove out of her way to pick up the pertinent issues of *Time* and *Newsweek*. To her, the threat of severe weather was as good as a promise. She had survived two close calls with tornadoes as a girl, one with toddler Roy in her arms. Both incidents remained vivid in her mind—they were two of the few childhood memories she ever mentioned. Roy remembered that Jean once offered another theory, that Phyl, without children to keep her young, had already progressed into the weather obsession found in many old ladies.

"I'm going to freeze the heart and kidneys for myself," Phyl said. "What do you want?"

Roy hated chicken. He had eaten nothing but growing up and secretly considered it white trash food.

"I'll make myself a sandwich," he replied.

"You need something hot," Phyl said.

"Soup, then. Don't start it, though. I'm going to lie down."

Flour blasted out of the bag as Phyl closed it. "I went out to the cemetery the other day to clean up Jean's grave. I found a bunch of pea plants."

"Peas?"

"I know peas when I see them," Phyl said with a nod. "A half dozen little sprouts. I pulled them up. The cemetery people don't let you to plant flowers, so I reckon vegetables aren't allowed."

"Maybe they blew over from a garden," Roy said.

"They wouldn't have all landed in the same place. I bet I can guess who planted them. I don't care, one way or the other, but I don't want him to expect them to be there when he visits."

Roy went up to Eric's room. They had not spoken much since the night with the coins. Or, rather, Eric had not answered questions with more than two or three words. Roy had begun to wonder about it. Like many parents he counted on the quick passing of those kinds of storms without grudges, though—again like many parents—he wrongly thought it involved forgiveness rather than the peculiar resilience of childhood that allowed a person to store such memories until he could recall them in adulthood and *then* hold a grudge.

Eric had piled his school clothes next to the door and changed into a pair of shorts and a striped shirt. He sat near the open window with his little thirty-dollar telescope pointed at the sky over the trees behind the well house.

"How was school?" Roy asked.

Eric did not turn around. "Okay."

"What about practice?"

"I hit fouls, like always," Eric said.

"Did the coach say anything about it?"

"No."

Roy fought back impatience, then spoke in the kindest voice he could manage. "Did you plant peas on your mother's grave?"

"Yes," Eric said.

"Why'd you do that, son?"

"Peas have nice flowers. At first, I mean. The little white ones."

"I know, I know."

"I can't buy flowers."

Roy watched him closely. "Phyl had to pull them up."

"Oh."

"There's a rule against planting things at the cemetery."

"Okay," Eric said. "They should let people, though. Like you could make plants grow on the tombstones. What's that stuff that's at Wrigley Field?"

"Ivy?" Roy said.

"You could put ivy on the tombstones. That way, they wouldn't look so creepy." Eric paused and looked out of the corner of his eye at his father. "Before you die," he went on, "you could say what you want to grow on top of your grave."

At first Roy stumbled over a response. "You don't have to worry about me dying for a while," he finally said.

Eric turned around. "You're sure?"

"I'm sure."

Suspicion played across Eric's face. Roy started to speak again, then backed off, and silently left the room. He glanced back. But Eric had returned to his telescope.

Not long after, Cowell arrived in a pickup. A scholar of the classifieds section, he had bought an upright freezer cheap from a family hoping to get all their worldly goods into a single U-Haul trailer. Roy helped Cowell set up the ramp. Eric and his sisters joined them.

"What is it?" Eric asked.

"It's a bubble machine," Cowell said.

"Really?"

"A bubble machine?" Cammy asked.

"Like on *Lawrence Welk*," Roy said.

Eric studied the freezer. "Do we need one?" he said.

"Of course you do," Cowell said. "Can't make champagne music without the bubble machine."

They used a dolly to prop up the freezer and, an inch at a time, rolled it down the ramp. Once at the bottom they put it down and sighed, less from exertion than relief at not losing it over the side of the ramp. The work gave Eric time to think up some follow-up questions.

"So where do the bubbles come out?" Eric asked.

"From the top," Roy replied. "You start the machine and open the lid, and then the bubbles float out."

"Is it going in the living room?" Eric said, unable to imagine a bubble machine anywhere else.

"In the basement," Roy said.

"Too noisy to put upstairs," Cowell added. "Once this mother gets revved up it sounds like a jet airplane. I'm not looking forward to taking her down those cellar steps. Hey, Eric. Do me a favor. Make sure there's beer waiting at the bottom."

Eric ran off to the refrigerator. Getting to the cellar door was the easy part. Roy took up a position with his shoulder against the freezer's side while Cowell, holding the dolly, leaned back like a farmer trying to restrain a horse determined to plow. As the freezer thumped onto each step Roy gave a grunt and paused to reset his feet.

"Should we help?" Eric said.

"Stay back," Roy gasped. "It's too heavy."

Veins stood out on Cowell's arms and neck. The dolly finally slid over the last step to the basement floor. He eased it down and with a wheeze draped himself over the top.

The pair steered the load toward the open electrical outlet in the laundry room. Just as they put the freezer down, Cammy let out a shriek. Roy, startled, lost his cigarette; Cowell spun to see her pointing at a mouse as it staggered across the floor. Taking aim, Cowell gave a little hop and brought the heel of his boot down on the mouse's head. Both Eric and Cammy let out howls and fled. Even Roy was surprised enough to delay the hunt for his cigarette.

"It wasn't moving too well," Cowell said thoughtfully. "Must've been poisoned." He looked in the direction Eric and Cammy had run. "You'd never know they were farm kids. Want me to clean it up?"

"I'll get it later," Roy said. "Let's finish with the bubble machine."

He plugged it in, Cowell fiddled with the settings, and the freezer roared to life.

"Loud or not the price was right," Cowell said. "Why don't we go outside and cool off?"

From the foot of the porch steps they watched Buck stalking rabbits out for an evening meal in the backyard. Birds sang at full volume. The sunset would be clear.

"The cat ever get one?" Cowell said in a low voice.

"Not that I know of," Roy answered.

Buck had just bent to pounce when the rabbits scattered.

"He's getting old," Roy said.

"I know the feeling," Cowell sighed. "Hey, did you read the paper yesterday?"

"I never get to it now that we're on overtime."

"I heard about the story first from Bobby Ladd. You know him? He's one of the deputies. But yesterday it got a big write-up. Sounds like a burglar broke into a house that's having some work done. The contractors found a hole in a wall to a secret room where the owner kept valuables, and it sounds like whoever went in stole a bunch of rare coins. Maybe you seen the place—it's the house that looks like George Washington lived there, over near the public golf course."

Roy stared straight ahead and Cowell, after pausing for a comment, continued.

"They called in the owner's son to ask what was missing, but he wasn't sure exactly, because I guess the old man didn't share the details of the collection with anyone else. As you can imagine those boys down at the sheriff's office are hot to investigate a real crime. I told Bobby the sheriff would have to let him take his bullet out of his pocket, though from the sound of it, the big man's taking charge personally."

Phyl called them for supper.

"That's something," Roy said to Cowell.

"Small-town crime wave," Cowell said. "Phyllis'll have me locking the doors."

ON ALTERNATE SATURDAYS the First Baptist Church hosted a flea market in the parking lot. Cowell always set up a table of treasures bought at estate sales and through the classifieds. Once in a while he sold something. When Phyl brought Eric from his baseball game to the church lot, she found most of the sellers—Cowell called them merchants—sprawled in lawn chairs, defeated by the heat. She pulled out without shopping. As a rule she divided flea market merchandise into two categories—junk and too expensive. Worst of all, one of the younger men set up near Cowell had covered a table with the most offensive collection of bumper stickers—marijuana leaves, *When this Van's a Rockin' Don't Come a Knockin'*, *OPEC Can Kiss My Ass*. She couldn't believe anyone was allowed to sell those kinds of things at a church.

As Eric approached, Cowell introduced him to Reverend Harlond. The reverend, an older man, wore a light-blue shirt, plaid pants, and a white belt with matching shoes—what Roy called preacher clothes.

"I'm looking into gold," the reverend said to Cowell. "They're legalizing the sale of it at the end of the year. I expect it'll be a good investment."

"Gold's always valuable," Cowell said, scratching at his hairier-bad-than-usual jaw. "Only one letter away from The Man himself, eh?" He slapped the reverend's shoulder.

"Gold's mentioned in the Bible," the reverend replied. "The stock market isn't, not that you'd know."

"The print in those Bibles is too small for me to read. The end of the year, you said?"

"You should look into it." The reverend thumbed toward the parking lot. "If business isn't too heavy, Cowell, I wondered if I could prevail on you to look at my radiator."

The flea market seldom netted Cowell any cash, but he dispensed a lot of valuable advice on automotive repair. He ordered Eric to watch the table and, still talking gold, shambled alongside the preacher in the general direction of a gray Buick. When he returned, Eric claimed he had an idea.

"You should answer questions about cars and make people pay you," he said.

"Yeah, probably," Cowell said. "But sometimes it's good to drum up a little goodwill. It's hot. Why don't you dig out the deck of cards from the cashbox, and we'll move to the shade. Business is going into a recessionary spiral anyway."

Eric dealt out a hand of Go Fish. To help with the heat Cowell pulled a couple of bottles of Dr Pepper from his Styrofoam cooler.

"Promise you won't cheat," Eric said.

"That hurts my feelings," Cowell said.

"You do cheat."

"Never have."

"How come you always win, then?"

"I'm just a good card player."

Eric could barely hold seven cards, and it never took long for him to tip them forward enough for Cowell to see. They went back and forth a few rounds, Cowell guessing wrong on purpose.

"Is Aunt Phyl leaving tomorrow?" Eric said.

"The car's all packed up," Cowell said.

"Do you have any kings?"

"Go fish. You looking forward to your Aunt Deb coming in?"

Eric concentrated for a moment on his cards. "Every time Aunt Deb comes there's a lot of arguing. Her and Dad, I mean. She's always bossing me around, too."

"She's trying to civilize you."

"What's that mean?"

"So's you don't eat with your hands the rest of your life. So's you don't go cutting farts at the movies. So's you're not a grown man going to smoky places with fast women or running off on those around-the-world voyages you read about."

"Is that stuff bad?" Eric said.

Cowell laughed and sat back. "There's hope for you yet. What I mean to say is, that's the sort of stuff you have to get out of your system before you can get domesticated."

"What's that?"

"Domesticated means you take something wild and beautiful and make it behave. You're showing me your cards again."

Eric jerked his hand close.

"See, when you're a man, you go through a crazy period in your life. It usually starts when you're, oh, about sixteen. Your Aunt Phyllis calls it high spirits. Some guys, it passes pretty fast. Others, it takes years, and some never give it up."

Eric looked quizzical.

"You remember at the family reunion?" Cowell asked. "When Will and Sam started blowing off those fireworks?"

"Mom wouldn't let me," Eric said, frowning.

"Those boys were too old for you. It was okay at first. They lit some firecrackers, set off a few of them rockets. Of course it got out of hand. It's bad enough they're seventeen without being Will and Sam. You throw in a bunch of their friends so they feel like showing off. . . ."

"They threw matches at each other," Eric said.

"With a pile of fireworks on the ground between them," Cowell exclaimed. He started his wheezy laugh, and the more he talked the harder he laughed. "I thought I was at Pearl Harbor. Damn. Those spinner things spitting fire all over the place. Then the bottle rockets blasting off in every direction. Thousands of firecrackers, whole bricks going off, *bang-bang-bang-bang.* Jesus. The whole bunch of them kids running around like their heads was on fire. I can still see them, screaming and waving their arms, and all of us hitting the deck and hiding under the picnic tables."

"Mom said it wouldn't be the Conlons unless some people got arrested."

Cowell began to simply wheeze. A minute later the laughter passed, and he took a deep breath.

"Brother, she had it right," he said, wiping his eyes. "I haven't been tickled like that in years. When I say you go through a crazy period, though, that's the sort of thing I mean, though later on it involves women and boozing and things."

"Will it happen to me?" Eric said.

"It happens to everybody in one way or another. Every man, at least. You got sevens?"

"Go fish. Aunt Deb says men cause most problems in the world."

"Well, that's probably true once you get outside the house. I reckon Deborah's a feminist."

"I don't know what that is," Eric said.

"Me neither. I didn't understand women before and I don't understand the new kind."

"Do you have kings?"

"You already asked that," Cowell said.

Without missing a beat Eric said, "Do you have jacks?"

Cowell chewed his lip to seem worried. He held all four, but he didn't like to discourage Eric by putting down a lot of points. "You got me," he said as he handed over clubs and spades.

CLOUDS ROLLED IN during the late afternoon. The change in the weather disappointed Eric. Of all his relatives—of everyone he knew, actually—Uncle Fergus alone showed any enthusiasm for astronomy. As Eric brooded over his bad luck, a Volkswagen bug skidded to a stop in front of the house. Strange music blasted from the car. As usual. According to Eric's father, Fergus listened to the weird music popular on college campuses.

Fergus squirmed out of the car like an astronaut abandoning an Apollo capsule. It took him longer than it took Aunt Deb. "Raw-boned," Cowell called him. "Doesn't that woman feed him?" asked Aunt Phyl. A tangle of wavy brown hair, ostensibly parted on the right (he depended on low winds to hold the part), seemed to stick out beyond his shoulders. Despite the muggy day he wore a checked flannel shirt. Mossy white thread dangled from the holes in his jeans.

"Hello, Dr. Copernicus," he said, bending down to Eric's eye level. "What's the buzz?"

"I'm okay," Eric said. Though he liked Uncle Fergus—and far more than Deb's previous husband—Eric only understood what he said about half the time.

Fergus removed his sunglasses, glanced at the sky. "Looks like a tough night for stargazing."

"Maybe it'll clear up," Eric said.

Deb leaned down, landed a kiss on Eric's cheek. "How are you, sweetheart? Why don't you help bring in the suitcases?"

"Ask her if she's a good tipper," Fergus said.

"No, I'm not," Deb replied over her shoulder.

"Where's Emma?" Eric said.

"At her dad's," Fergus said. "She has another week of school."

That was a break, as far as Eric was concerned. Most of the

time Emma ignored him in favor of her books or the grown-ups, but not until after she had thrown a fit because he played board games the wrong way.

Eric accompanied Fergus around the bug, paused to read the bumper sticker. On the left was a picture of Albert Einstein in front of a field of stars. Next to it the blue letters said:

186,000 miles per second
IT'S THE LAW.

The speed of light, Eric said to himself. He felt a flush of excitement at his knowledge.

Leaning into the car, he noticed a coffee can in the backseat. "That's for you," Fergus said. Eric looked first at the wide bottom —Sagittarius, he thought. On the can's side was a picture of an Arab drinking coffee from a bowl.

The Arabs believed parts of Sagittarius to be many things, a ladle and an ostrich nest among them. Eric nodded to himself. If the coffee company put an Arab on the side, he figured he should devote the can to a constellation on which the Arabs had an opinion.

The music played on. The aurora was rising behind the guy singing. Eric veered aside to the eight-track.

"Can I look at your tape?" he asked.

"Sure. Do you like the music?"

Eric pulled the tape out. A scruffy guy's face filled most of the cover.

"I didn't hear very much," Eric answered.

"My students keep me hip," Fergus said. "I'd never find bands on my own. Only bachelors have time to keep up with rock and roll."

Fergus took the suitcases. Eric handled Deb's makeup and toiletries bags. When they got inside she was sitting at the dining room table talking to Roy while the girls pressed hands against her stomach. A short time later the men and their beers stood at the grill near the kitchen porch. Roy, out of lighter fluid, used gasoline to start the fire. It ignited with an impressive mushroom cloud.

Roy also preferred Fergus to the first husband. David had been chronologically ten years older than Roy, but his stiff formality tempted Roy to count those as dog years. Fergus, by contrast, was a year younger. Roy felt uncomfortable with someone of his education, particularly as Fergus edged toward becoming an assistant professor and, as he had over the last year, published a few short stories. From the go, however, Fergus took to the kids, unfazed by Cammy's handicap or Eric's initial shyness. Roy gave him a lot of credit for it.

"Out of school yet?" Roy said.

"For a couple weeks," Fergus said. "Then the summer session starts."

"Still writing?"

Fergus chuckled an embarrassed laugh. "Trying science fiction."

"Nothing wrong with that," Roy said. "Look at *Star Trek*. Been cancelled for years and it's still on TV."

The family sat down to hamburgers, canned corn, and a green bean casserole the kids insisted should be adults-only. Mr. Johnson, sure of Grub's drops, circled the table in defiance of Deb's attempts to shoo him away. At one point Cammy asked if Aunt Phyl had arrived in Missouri. Roy said she had.

"It's a long trip," Eric said.

"You remember the last time you went down there?" Roy said.

"Aunt Lucy had that stuff in her lip."

"Chaw. Yeah. Some of the old ladies still dip. Bet you never saw anything like that."

"I wouldn't want to see it," Deb said.

"I like it because it lets you spit in the house," Fergus said.

"Yeah," Eric said.

"This is inappropriate for the dinner table," Deb said.

"Lucy keeps it civilized," Roy insisted. "She spits in her coffee can."

Eric said, "I remember when Cammy tried to drink out of her can."

The look on Deb's face caused Fergus to choke with laughter.

"Shit, I'd forgotten that," Roy said.

"Mom was pretty mad," Eric said.

"Nah. Just surprised." He glanced at Deb, then said to Eric, "I don't think there's too many Aunt Lucys on her side of the family."

"Can we talk about something else, please?" Deb said.

Eric led Fergus upstairs after supper. They sat on the floor of Eric's room with the pile of constellations, two bottles of pop, and a napping Mr. Johnson between them. Eric explained he wanted to save the south circumpolar constellations until last. Working on those exotic shapes was to be the reward for getting so close to the finish of his project.

Fergus received this explanation with exaggerated gravity. "Which ones are the south circumpolar constellations?" he asked.

"The ones that are visible in the Southern Hemisphere every night of the year," Eric said. He chanted the list while pointing to each on the star map. Southern Cross. Centaur. Flying Fish and Goldfish. Peacock and Toucan. Carina, keel of the ship *Argo*. Eric also noted the fuzzy blue blotches of the Magellanic Clouds, mentioned that the nearby galaxies were famously observed by the old boot eater himself.

"Do you know the story of the *Argo*?" Fergus said.

"No."

"It's from Greek mythology. Have you ever heard of Jason and the Argonauts? Maybe you've seen the movie version."

"Is it about astronomy?" Eric said.

"Man, it's an adventure story. The hero, Jason, is the king of a Greek city, but this bad guy has stolen the throne. He cons Jason into taking on a quest to retrieve the Golden Fleece, a magic sheepskin made of gold. Jason knows there's going to be monsters galore in the way, so he puts together a crew of famous all-star heroes to help him. They even get Hercules to come along."

"He's a constellation, too," Eric exclaimed.

"See, you know part of it. In the movie, though, Hercules doesn't look like a hero. He's more like a fat guy with an old rug that's supposed to be a lion skin. Fortunately, the Greek gods are helping out. The goddess Hera helps Jason equip a magic ship called the *Argo*. On the back of it there's a talking statue she uses to pass along advice to Jason. The sailors, the Argonauts, sail out to sea and get hassled everywhere they go. Iron giants, Harpies, skeletons jumping out of the earth, this dragon-thing with multiple heads called the Hydra—man. It's a real good time."

"Does he get the gold sheepskin?" Eric said.

"You don't want me to ruin it for you, do you?"

Fergus paused to listen for the sound of conversation from downstairs. As he was tuning in he noticed a newspaper ad with a picture of Albert Einstein tacked in one corner of Eric's bulletin board. Einstein had his tongue sticking out. It seemed the great physicist had been recruited to pitch for a local used record store.

"Do you like Einstein?" Fergus asked.

"He invented $E = mc^2$," Eric said.

"I don't know if he invented it. It's more like he discovered it. Don't tell me they're teaching the theory of relativity in third grade."

"We're still on long division," Eric said with a sour expression.

"Do you know what $E = mc^2$ means?"

"Go around the world and there's only a dozen people who really understand $E = mc^2$," Fergus said. "It's an equation to express the nature of energy, more or less. Physicists use it to understand stuff like black holes."

"How do they use it?" Eric asked.

"Beats me. I'm not one of those dozen people."

"But don't you write whole long books about science?"

Fergus gave a rueful laugh. "I'm a science fiction writer, Eric. Most of us don't know anything about real science."

"That's a hell of an idea," Roy said.

Deb leaned back in her chair, spent from her speech and sweating from the humidity.

Small class size, annual science fair, diverse student population, campaigning for scholarships and grants—he was still trying to catch up. To aid the process he concentrated on lighting a cigarette. Was this a genuine opportunity, as she said? Or an insinuation Eric could do better elsewhere? She wanted to uproot him now, after everything that had happened to his family in the past six months?

"You're aware Eric lives *here*, right?" Roy asked.

Deb answered with a pursing of the lips.

"I don't know," he said. "It hasn't been that long since Jean's funeral. Having to make new friends again, all the instability—he's just finished third grade and he's already been to four different schools. I don't know about sending him to another one, and on top of that in a big city. I don't think Eric's ever seen traffic."

"He won't be driving," Deb said.

"It's too much change."

They sat quiet a moment, listening to competing music—the crickets outside the screen door versus the hum of Eric's radio.

"If we act quickly," Deb said, "at least Eric has the option. I'm proposing that we look into the possibility."

Roy gestured at her stomach with his cigarette. "You want two new kids?"

"I can handle Eric."

Since Jean's death, in fact, Deb had many times considered the possibility of *four* new kids. Having heard about Roy's last bender from Cammy only reaffirmed her fears. In moments of clarity she chalked up the visions of that dystopia to morbid feelings that still lingered from Jean's death. Rather than struggle to unknot those fears, however, Deb spent her sleepless late hours imagining new tragedies to overcome, new problems to solve, preferring even dreadful fantasies to the kind of bracing reality she faced in this house so unchanged—save in one way—with Jean's tchotchkes still tumbled on the shelves, her music still in the air, her moods still animating the faces of her children.

Roy, suspecting his first excuses had found no traction, said, "If he doesn't get financial help, I don't see how we'll come up with the tuition money."

He'll get in if I have to build his classroom with my own hands, she thought. "You'll consider it?"

"I need him here."

"To do what? Bring in the harvest?"

"He keeps an eye on the girls, for one thing," Roy said.

"Someone should be keeping an eye on him."

"That isn't possible all the time."

Deb stood. "Will you consider it, or not?"

"Look into it if you want," he said. "No promises, though."

That seemed to satisfy her. Deb went into the kitchen. A few moments later he heard water drumming against the bottom of the teakettle. He knew from experience that with Deb mere verbal agreement sufficed, to be used as leverage at a future decisive moment—everything was lawyering with her. He figured he was lucky to get out without having to sign a contract. Maybe she would give up on the idea, though Deb, like Jean, rarely gave up. Maybe Eric would fail to get in. Neither of these thoughts were hopes, exactly. Neither could be, not if you loved your son. Not if you were capable of shame.

On Monday, Roy worked on the second floor of some apartment houses. Being partnered with the laconic Fraser gave him time to think, and he welcomed thoughts of something other than the coins. He tried to rehearse indignation and decisiveness to use with Deb, for a little while convinced himself he could use both to bury this idea she had sprung on him; but years of sparring with Jean made him wary of the dangers of confrontation, and by the end of the workday he had abandoned the strategy in favor of the more reliable practice of delaying until deadlines passed. The pocket veto, the prevent defense.

Not that he admitted it to himself. The thought that he had a strategy arose only once, insisting on the need for planning, calculation; but he banished it from his conscious mind. Because you couldn't admit you wanted to run out the clock. Not if you loved your son. Not if you were capable of shame.

ALREADY ROY WAS a half hour late getting home. The instinct to work off the growing tension seemed to catch. On the way downstairs Eric glanced at Fergus writing in a spiral notebook in the study. Outside, Mr. Johnson hobbled off after the rabbits, scattering mothers and kittens in all directions. Deb banged through the kitchen porch to hang linen on the clothesline. The sheets billowed like sails, and Eric wished he could head out to sea with Magellan.

He went to the garden but again gave up on using the hoe. It was too big, even when he choked up. Instead he pulled weeds by hand, though indifferently, only bothering with the biggest. The first radishes and carrots were well underway. Buds nestled under the leaves on the pepper plants. The first bright-green leaves of the watermelon canopy had opened on the vines. The kite string they had used to plan the rows was long gone, blown into the shrubbery like ruined spiderwebs. But he admired the rows' straight lines. They had done as good a job as the farmers who used machinery, and almost as good as Aunt Phyl.

Deb waved him over. "What's that rash?" she asked.

He submitted to scrutiny of the reddened skin on his left calf and knee, the back of his neck up under his ear, and a thumb-sized patch that had appeared that morning beside his right eye. Past skin problems had trained Eric to rub the skin rather than use his nails, and he had thus far avoided the usual long scabby scratches. Deb claimed there were red blotches under his chin and on his right arm. During the subsequent bath they found further inflammation on the insides of both legs.

"When did this happen?" she exclaimed.

"It started a couple days ago," Eric said.

"Where did you get it?"

Eric shrugged but under questioning he conceded he knew the rash was unusual. He explained he kept it secret because he refused to wear the clown makeup again. The clown makeup, Deb gathered through the subsequent tears, was the medicine used to treat his case of impetigo a couple of years before. Everyone made fun of him when he wore it, he said. The idea of going to baseball practice with purple paint on his face horrified him. He wouldn't do it.

After the bath Deb dabbed calamine lotion on his legs. Eric screamed when she even mentioned putting some on his face, so she returned the bottle to the cabinet. That done, she concentrated on his hair, brushed it flat against his head. Too hard, as usual, to Eric's mind. He told her that her hair, and Emma's, was thick and dark. It could take a brush whereas his finer hair easily surrendered and let the teeth rake his scalp. The explanation got him nowhere.

By the time she freed him the sun was down. The clear skies offered an excellent chance to use the telescope. On his way to get Fergus he heard music coming. Halfway up the stairs he recognized "Smackwater Jack," by Carole King. Eric whipped around the corner into the study.

"Hey," he exclaimed. "That's Carole King!"

Fergus gave a yelp. For a moment he fumbled with, and then dropped, his notebook. "Jesus," he said, a hand against his chest. "That jack-in-the-box routine is going to kill me."

"Sorry. That's Carole King. Do you like her?"

Fergus twisted around, propped his feet up on the bed. "She's more Aunt Deb's thing," he said. "We're on our second copy of that record."

"Do you like the picture?" Eric said.

"What picture?"

"On the cover."

"Sure," Fergus said as he studied the photo. "Don't tell me you're into Carole King."

"I wrote her a letter," Eric said.

"She's a bit old for you."

"You're a writer, right?"

"I labor under that pretension," Fergus said.

"Why don't you talk like a normal person? So if you're a writer, you know how to write letters, too."

"Sure. Show me what you wrote first, though."

A moment later Eric returned with a spiral notebook. He flipped past the lists of star names and constellation drawings and settled on a note written in his most careful cursive lettering. Fergus received it with the solemnity required at an important occasion.

"Dear Mrs. King," the letter began.

"I'm not sure if she's a miss or missus," Eric said.

"I think she's a miss at present," Fergus said. "When you're not sure, use *Ms.* That works with everyone but old ladies."

"I am writing to say I like your album and I want to ask a few questions."

Now Eric had swung around behind Fergus to read along. "Our teacher," he said, "told us to start a letter by stating very clearly what it's about."

"No offense, but are you going to let me read?"

"Okay, read."

> My mom used to listen to *Tapestry* a lot. She died last year of cancer. I still listen to your record, though. Here are my questions.
>
> 1: What is the name of your cat?
>
> 2: Do you still knit?
>
> 3: Do you still live in New York?
>
> 4: Are you ever coming to Illinois?
>
> I don't think you will answer. If you do, you will be better than E.B. White. Thank you for your time.

> Sincerely,
> Eric Conlon

"What do you have against E.B. White?" Fergus said.

Eric made a face. "So do you think it's a good letter?"

"I'm sure she doesn't get these questions every day."

"What's bad is, I don't know where to send a letter to her."

"Yeah," Fergus said. "She doesn't seem like the kind of person with a fan club, exactly. Sometimes people send letters to an artist's agent or their record company. You could try that." He contemplated the amount of mail going into either of those destinations and tripped his mental circuit breakers. "Actually, let me think about it. The information must be available. You don't mind waiting while I check into it, do you?"

"Can you get the address of her house?" Eric said.

"Man, you aim high. Considering how *Tapestry* sold, she might be living at the Taj Mahal. I'll do some research. There may be a reference book with celebrity addresses."

The slam of the screen door cut off Eric's next question. Too-loud laughter followed too-loud hellos.

Fergus lifted the arm of the record player. Seeing Eric rooted in place, he paused, said, "Don't you want to go downstairs?"

"Not yet," Eric whispered.

At the sound of boots on the stairs Eric's face began to burn. Very casually Fergus lay back, propped his feet up, feigned interest in the afternoon's writing. The electronic buzz from the record player speakers filled the room. Eric turned away from the door.

Roy arrived in the doorway, a wide grin on his face, unsure enough of his balance that he leaned. "Hey, boys, what's going on?" he exclaimed. "Thought you'd be out with the telescope, or whatever the hell that thing is."

Fergus could see Eric was not only too embarrassed to speak, but so mortified he could not even move. Holding up his notebook, Fergus returned Roy's broad smile—sacrificing sincerity for obviousness, the way he did at conferences—and said, "Just working on the book."

"Looks like you're working hard," Roy said loudly. Like a lot of drunks, Roy had difficulty adjusting his amplification. While Fergus smiled at the good-natured tone of the words, he heard the insincerity volleyed back at him.

"Well, Eric here's helping me with the astronomy stuff," Fergus said.

"Eric?" Roy said. Eric did not answer. In fact, at that moment Eric believed that if he did not move or speak he might become invisible, the way certain animals did on *Wild Kingdom.* "What's wrong with you?" Roy exclaimed. A different shade of red began to rise in Roy's face. "Is this all you do? Sit around talking about astronomy bullshit?" When Eric still remained rigid Roy's voice rose to a yell. "Jesus, you're just like your mother. Except your mother—you know, why don't you take him to the city, Fergus? You're obviously a great parent." Neither replied. Roy glared at each, then made a loud growling sound and turned away. His first step nearly took him down the staircase; only animal instinct jerked out his hand to grab the rail. "Do what you want," he said in a stage mumble. "Who gives a fuck?"

His footsteps thumped down the stairs. For a moment Fergus awaited the inevitable slip and fall. There was a crash—Roy had knocked a picture off the wall, then came to rest at the bottom with a huge sigh. This was followed by more mumbling, which was cut off by the slamming of the bathroom door.

Fergus leaned over and tousled Eric's damp hair.

"It's all right," he said. "Will he go to sleep soon?"

"Probably," Eric said.

"You shouldn't listen to him about the astronomy. That's a total drag, talking about it that way. When he sobers up he won't even remember he saw us." Eric nodded, wiped his eyes. "You scared?"

"No," Eric said.

The red in Eric's cheeks was more luminous than the rash. Fergus realized he was embarrassed.

"Once he crashes we'll take the telescope out and see what's going on in the universe," he said.

Deb began screaming the moment the bathroom door swung open. At first Roy mumbled that he wanted to go to bed. She started with a thick sarcasm Fergus recognized. For a moment the fight moved away from the stairs. Someone pounded on the table so hard the windows rattled. The girls began to keen.

"I'd better go save my wife," Fergus said to Eric. "Though it may turn out I'm saving him. Stay up here."

But Eric followed, waiting until Fergus turned the corner at the bottom of the stairs before making his own quiet descent.

Fergus lingered for a moment on the fringes. He hoped his presence would defuse one and preferably both of them. To his surprise Roy appeared confused as Deb told him how he'd embarrassed and terrified his children. Fergus stepped between them,
tried to quiet her long enough for Roy to save face and go off
to bed. When Roy rebounded on her, leaning in so that his face
almost touched hers, Fergus turned toward him, still murmuring for calm, and then Roy took him by the shirt and flung him
across the dining room table. One table leg snapped. Vase, toys,
and silverware careened into a heap on the floor. Fergus, trying to
catch himself, tumbled over the chair on the opposite side. Both
he and the chair clattered into the wall.

Stunned, and for the moment upside-down, Fergus paused to
make sure everything worked. Roy stood over the scene a moment,
tottering from foot to foot. Finally he stumbled back a step. He
shouldered open the screen door. A moment later Eric heard the
Ford start. Roy scattered gravel and took off down the driveway.

Behind him he heard Fergus say, "You should've stopped him,
Deb. He's driving drunk."

"He drove drunk to get home, didn't he?" she cried.

Fergus got to his feet. He called out through the commotion of
tears and screaming, asking for calm, saying nothing was broken
except the table.

In a half hour the house was quiet again. Eric prepared to go
outside with his star guide and flashlight. He called Mr. Johnson
in a hushed voice and, leaving his shoes behind, tiptoed down
the porch steps. The wet sidewalk felt cool. He scraped his bare
toes across the rough surface, smiled at the good feeling. Stars
glimmered where the lingering clouds had parted. Eric stood in
the center of the yard and shook from immense relief, a relief
unsurpassed even by the ancient Chinese when their bells and
gongs drove off the dragon eating the sun. The Sickle of Leo was
tipping toward the western horizon. Boötes towered overhead.
To the east Vega glimmered from atop diamond-shaped Lyra between the spans of two trees.

A little while later Fergus joined him.

"What do you see?" Fergus asked.

"The Big Dipper."

"Even an amateur like me can see that. What do *you* see?"

"I was looking between the stars," Eric said. "Do you think anything is there?"

"In the black part?" Fergus said.

"Yeah."

"What's your opinion?"

Eric stared into the star-poor area south of Ursa Major. Canes Venatici, the Hunting Dogs, stalked that part of the sky.

"I think maybe there's stars in the black parts, but they're too far away for us to see," Eric said. "Like when you can see more stars with a telescope than with just your eyes. So there must be stars you can't see even with a telescope. Right?"

"Logical."

"But if you sent a rocket straight from Earth to that spot, straight ahead I mean, you'd hit a star someday. Maybe. Or the stars are too new, and the light hasn't reached Earth yet, so it only looks empty, but it isn't."

"You're blowing my mind," Fergus said.

"Though the books say space is mostly empty, so maybe there's nothing there."

Fergus paused, out of respect, then said what he'd come out to say. "Your uncle Cowell called. Your dad's at his place."

"That's where he goes," Eric said, nodding.

"Weren't you worried?"

"No," Eric said. "My mom used to cry, but Dad's always all right. Uncle Cowell says God protects drunks."

FERGUS HAD BEEN a confirmed night owl in his bachelor days. Once married, however, he had incentives to change his ways. First, Deb was a morning person. His chances for lovemaking peaked around 6 a.m. and steadily fell to nil around nine in the evening. As the promise of steady lovemaking was one of the reasons he married, Fergus felt he should play the percentages. Second, early morning offered the opportunity to write in quiet. He used the time for brainstorming and working in his notebooks, and the noisier afternoon for the less Muse-driven work of banging on the typewriter.

The creaky hideaway bed reported Fergus turning over to get up. In a burst of wishful thinking he went to the study's single small window to see if dawn was far enough away to let him sleep a little more. But from the looks of it the sun had risen a half hour earlier.

"Do you want me to make you coffee?" Deb mumbled. "They have this tricky old coffee pot."

"I can figure it out," Fergus said. "The percolator I used in grad school brewed the coffee that washed down the Donner Party. Promise me you won't smother Roy in his sleep."

"He's home?"

"He came in about three."

Deb rolled over onto one elbow. "Are you okay?"

"Better than the table," Fergus said.

"Seriously."

"I'm being serious." Fergus patted her on the behind. "Let me work. Go to sleep."

Fergus went downstairs to the kitchen and spooned up enough coffee to make it strong—he'd slept badly and had a drive back to the city ahead of him. With the dining room table *hors de combat,* he set up in the kitchen. Shortly after sunrise he heard someone coming downstairs. None of the kids possessed the weight to make the stairs creak so loudly.

Roy banged around the kitchen, went to the bathroom, let the dog out and the cat in. It was ten minutes before he said, "I didn't mean what I said."

"Sure you did. Booze is the poor man's truth serum." Without looking up Fergus pointed to the counter with his pen. "There's coffee if you want it."

DOMBEY RETURNED TO the work site that morning. The look he exchanged with Roy said they would talk. At lunch he announced a run to the convenience store. Roy told Tiny he had an errand. Ten minutes later he met Dombey in the store's parking lot.

"We can't stay long," Dombey said as they went inside. "It'd look suspicious."

"To who?" Roy asked.

Dombey led him around a candy rack to the freezers. "It's possible someone's watching. I don't know for sure. I've got a feeling."

"Why did you call the fucking cops?"

"It was a preemptive strike. The Judge's son was going to visit the house. If he'd found the stuff gone who do you think the cops would've busted? This way, we look like good citizens. I've got a story."

"We need to sell the stuff," Roy hissed.

Dombey stiffened. An ugly expression replaced the friendly one. "It's just a delay," he said. "This asshole knows the pressure's on us, and he thinks he can sweat us for less money. We wait him out, let him get an even bigger hard-on for the coins, and it'll be fine."

"How long does that take?"

"Do I look like a goddamn fortune-teller?"

Roy felt the world spinning. "Can't we put the coins back?"

"Are you nuts? This isn't first grade. There's no take-backs. Put it back. Jesus, then they'd know for sure it was us. Who else could get in twice?" Dombey took a deep breath. "Prison's full of people who lose their cool, Roy. And that can't happen. One of us goes down, we all go, you understand?"

"You take the stuff."

"Fuck that," Dombey said. "You're getting a third of ten grand because they won't suspect you."

Roy wondered what had happened to the fifteen, maybe twenty grand.

"You can have my share," Roy said.

"I don't want your share. I want mine and I can't get it without you."

Roy had often bent under the weight of his regrets, but none was so heavy as whatever series of circumstances had led him to put his life in Carl Dombey's hands.

"I want the stuff out of my house," Roy whispered.

"Just stay cool," Dombey said, and a hint of camaraderie returned to his voice. "It'll take a few extra days. That's all. I guarantee you, this stalling tactic is harder on him than it is on us."

THE CEMETERY WAS NESTLED in the elbow of a sharp turn in the highway. A few dozen bleached slats stood at the edge of a cornfield, the resting place of founders and farmers and the children of each taken young by pneumonia or scarlet fever. Two majestic sycamores shaded them. Alongside the narrow footpath leading to the historic section stood a marker explaining how the cemetery site had been chosen, how an early town father used his money and spare time to see that it conformed to the standards of the Victorian Age. Families held picnics under the trees and records showed two wedding ceremonies had taken place on the grounds.

At a certain time of the afternoon—the hour and minute depending on the day of the year—the marker's shadow fell across Jean's grave.

Deb removed the wrapping from her flowers and spread them before the headstone. From the weather report she guessed they would be washed away in a matter of hours. She remembered, as she always did when Jean crossed her mind, the image of her sister in the intensive care ward, hair wet with sweat, her face frightened for the first time in her life, her body reduced to the bells and whistles of the machine that sustained her. When she choked, the monitor watching her gag reflex gave a piercing beep. Fifteen minutes at the bedside nearly destroyed their aunt Fran; and even Deb only built up her resistance to the shock by allowing her own frequent visits to finally melt into a vigil. It was like watching a natural feature of the landscape inexplicably crumble away in the face of some fantastic and unforeseen disaster. Deb could remember Jean in other places and in other times, but when thinking of her she first had to pass the sickbed, always, as if the broken doll Jean became guarded the vault holding her memories.

Grub pulled on Deb's sleeve. "Okay, we'll go," Deb said. In the car she checked her purse for cash, coupons, and Roy's wad of food stamps. On the way she vetoed all the girls' requests for what to buy. "I'm disturbed that a large part of your vocabulary consists of product names," she added to Grub.

Deb picked items off the shelf like a junkman in a hurry. Old ladies blanched as the cart barreled toward them. In the meat department she tossed in a few steaks and a roast and, despite her own low opinions of the cuts, numerous packages of cube steak and round steak. She referred to her list only for those animal parts used in Roy's meat-and-bean dishes. Cammy consulted on the popularity of specific brands of breakfast cereal, and while she annoyed Deb by asking for every item that contained chocolate, she did remind her to buy more calamine lotion. In produce she picked up a bag of potatoes and only at the last second remembered the frozen peas.

In the checkout line Grub turned whiny and Cammy persisted in rifling through the candy display. Deb dug out all her forms of currency. She knew, in theory, that food stamps came with limitations, but she had no idea what they might be. Best to just throw them on the belt and let the cashier do the sorting. Then she heard a whisper behind her.

Deb turned and stopped short, stunned by the women's appearance. The older of the two wore a floral-pattern shirt and pastel-colored slacks; the younger, obviously her daughter, flew the colors of a local high school on her T-shirt and wore white shorts down to two hammy knees. What really caught Deb off-guard, however, were the matching beehives.

"Excuse me?" she said as she took it all in.

They glared at her, the food on the belt, her again.

Deb tossed a handful of food stamps at the older woman, causing her to hold up her hands and stagger back. When the daughter started to speak, Deb rammed the cart into her, swatted the round steak off the belt and toward her head, launched into the profanity she usually used on maniac cabbies. A manager rushed over. His pleas for calm failed to halt the barrage of curses until he wedged his body between Deb and the cart of the women behind her. He begged the woman in the high school T-shirt to escort her mother to a newly opened line two lanes over. When the scene had ended, the manager pushed Deb's cart to the car for her and personally loaded the trunk. To his great relief the mother in the pastel pants had parked at the opposite end of the lot. Both women cast dark looks at Deb on the way to their car.

"I hope your store doesn't have a problem with food stamps," Deb said, hands on her hips.

"No, ma'am," the manager said. "We take them the same as cash or check."

Deb held out a five but the manager shook his head. "For the trouble," she added.

"No trouble, ma'am," he replied. "I'm used to it. Shoot, I took less abuse from my football coach in high school."

HE LOOKED LIKE A MONSTER NOW. Poison ivy had caused the rash, and with help from Eric's scratching hands it had spread everywhere. Scabs crusted pink with layers of calamine lotion covered half his forehead, hooked around his left eye across his cheek and down to the corner of his mouth. Aunt Deb had already predicted that his eyebrows might be pulled out when the scabs finally fell away. Scabs also covered his nostrils, meaning that in addition to the constant itching all over his body he always had to flick flakes of dead skin out of his nose. The least amount of sweat irritated the rash on his neck and arms. The past few nights he awakened numerous times and tried to quell the itch by rubbing the areas through his sheets. Every time he pulled off a loose scab in the hopes the skin had healed underneath he instead saw bright blotches. If it did not heal in the next few days he would have to go to the doctor. The thought of showing up for a baseball game in the medicinal clown paint made Eric's stomach burn.

He hopped down from the sink, let out Mr. Johnson, and then followed him into the yard. Tossing the ball in the hot sun would bring on more sweat-induced torment, but he couldn't think of anything else to do. The garden looked okay. He was stuck on which constellation to do next. When Deb was leaving for the store, he promised to stick to a list of agreed-upon activities, one of which was playing ball. Veering from the list might jeopardize the privilege of staying home alone. A lot of kids his age—older, even—were not allowed to do so and suffered through all the parental errands. Johnny Garland was in *sixth grade*, yet never stayed home alone. The Garlands had tried that experiment with him the previous summer. Eric remembered overhearing Mrs. Garland tell his mother that Johnny stuffed the oven with fireworks. "I guess he's just a boy," she had added, with her ever-present smile.

Sweat ran down Eric's face, despite his standing in the shade. The sunlight heating him was about seven minutes old. Thousands of years from now, that same light would reach distant planets at 186,000 miles per second. It was the law. According to Fergus, many scientists believed that everything happened at once at the speed of light—past, present, and future. This was a theory, an idea, in this case Einstein's, about how space and time worked. As yet no one could prove it true except using the math that next to no one understood, one reason being that human beings, as yet, had no machines capable of light speed. Eric tried to imagine standing on a beam of light. "It's kind of hard to understand," Fergus had warned, "but you'd be all stretched out, one long Eric, like a freight train, the baby Eric on one end, the elderly Eric on the other. Every moment that happened to you would be happening to you, all at once."

"Again?" Eric had asked.

Not exactly again, Fergus had said. That implied a past and present. At the speed of light, the past and present happened at the same time. You stood in every place you had ever stood, and at every time, too. "Including the time you're standing at the speed of light?" Eric had wondered. "Now you're blowing my mind again," Fergus had answered.

Eric, though unclear on the particulars, thought the speed of light sounded pretty nice. There were several moments he wanted to see again. Or not again, exactly. Anyway, whatever Fergus meant. Often he forgot what he read and had to look it up again. At the speed of light he could remember it all. And he would pay money for a replay of his cousins setting off that pile of fireworks. Of course if he knew everything from all times in his life, he could use his seven-year-old self to warn Mom to visit the doctor in time to catch the cancer. Maybe he could get back some lost memories, too. Ever since the funeral it had become harder to remember more than a dozen or so specific times with her. The baseball game when he was beaned in the head. The time she missed Dad with a thrown pan and instead put it through the living room window. Being dropped off at Akhmatova for the first time. The hospital. The wake. He knew there were more. Maybe the poison ivy was punishment for forgetting. Aunt Phyl said God punished people for bad deeds.

Roy called just after four o'clock. Storms had driven his crew into a waffle house near the construction site. From the window over the sink Deb could see black clouds rising along the western horizon. She turned on the radio on the windowsill, leaned against the sink to wait for the next weather report.

"Eric? Honey?" Deb called. "They're giving storm watches on the radio. Is Lee County near us?"

"That way," Eric said, pointing west.

She turned to look. "It's definitely dark."

"Is it a severe thunderstorm watch or a tornado watch?"

"Both. It's a warning in some places."

"Is it a warning for Lee or Ogle?"

Impressive, Deb thought. "Yes to both."

"Then the storm is probably going to come here," Eric said.

Deb finished mixing up a pitcher of punch, collected Grub, and changed her diaper. As she was going outside to clear the clothesline Buck darted from his napping place on the step to the kitchen porch and bounded into the kitchen.

"We can't hear the sirens if they go off," Eric called from the fence separating the garden from the cornfield.

Deb shaded her eyes. "Do you go downstairs every time there's a storm, then?"

"Not every time," Eric said as he walked toward her. "If Aunt Phyl's here, we go. With my dad it's only sometimes. I think this storm might be bad, though."

"Why?"

"Because Buck ran into the house. He's got weather ESP. No, he does. Aunt Phyl says animals can predict bad storms."

Racing black clouds soon covered the sun. Curtains billowed at every window. The wind chimes hanging on the porch tinkled one moment, trilled in the rising breeze the next. Through the kitchen window Deb saw a brown dust devil in the distance. At first she mistook it for the greater storm, an infant tornado, but, seeing it dissipate, realized the wind along the front had kicked it up. A first growl of thunder rattled the windows.

There's something in the air, she said to herself.

Buck thought so, too. He stood next to the stove, alert.

At the next sound of thunder Grub rushed in and attached herself to Deb's left leg. Deb called for the other kids as she scooped Grub into her arms. Eric arrived at a run.

"Do you have a family plan of some kind?" Deb asked.

"A what?"

"A plan, Eric. Like the fire safety plans you do at school? What do you do when you go down to the basement?"

Eric opened one of the drawers next to the sink. "We take the transistor radio," he said, pointing. "And the flashlight, too, because sometimes the power goes off. I already put the lawn chairs downstairs so we'll have something to sit on."

Another louder rumble of thunder passed overhead. Grub covered her ears. Twilight had fallen. Bending as her belly allowed, craning her neck while simultaneously trying not to knock heads with Grub, Deb peered out the window overlooking the yard, saw dark clouds perilously low to the ground, and a white-pink flash to the west.

"Go ahead of me, Cammy," Deb ordered. "Hurry up. Use the rail."

Mr. Johnson leapt ahead of Deb and trotted down the steps. "Goddamn dog," Deb said. "Eric?"

No answer.

"Eric?" she called.

"I have to get something," he said, already far away.

"Should we open the windows?"

"They're already open."

The screen door on the kitchen porch clapped against the house.

"Don't forget the radio," Cammy said.

"I'm trying not to forget your brother," Deb said. "Eric, right now."

He leapt over the last few stairs just as she finished, skidded into the kitchen in his stocking feet, and added the transistor radio and flashlight to the star guide and shoebox of baseball cards already cradled in his arm. At the bottom of the basement steps he took a seat on the edge of the reclining lawn chair to catch his breath.

"Is there anything else we should be doing?" Deb asked.

Eric said, "Dad told us we should hide under his tool bench for when the house collapses."

"When the house collapses," she repeated. What little she knew of tornadoes she had learned from Eric, and at the moment all she recalled were bits of freakish folklore, the wind-driven straw sticking from trees, for instance, and the flying cows.

"At least your father had enough foresight to move you out of the mobile home," she added.

"We forgot Dusty," Cammy said.

They crisscrossed the basement searching for the cat. Calls and smooching sounds only brought forth Buck and Mr. Johnson.

"Well, he'll be okay," Deb said.

In a matter of seconds Cammy and Grub were as despondent as paid mourners. Somewhere upstairs a lamp blew over, startling all of them, and the girls screamed for Dusty at an even higher pitch, heedless of Deb's comforting murmurs or her follow-up shouts for quiet.

"I can get him," Eric offered.

"Goddamn cat," Deb said. "Stay here."

She climbed the steps, one hand on the rail, the other supporting the bulge of the baby. At the top she threw the latch on the door and the house's powerful cross drafts whipped it open with a loud bang. Her curses sounded through the house, and the kids looked up in surprise as they heard a chair skid across the floor and clatter into the counter. None of them believed the wind had moved it. Dusty, as predicted, was crouched behind the refrigerator. No smooching noises remained in the heart or on the lips of his rescuer. Instead, Deb seized a broom and tried to shoo him free with the handle. When that failed she screamed a string of curses and shouldered the corner of the refrigerator away from the wall. Dusty dashed through the kitchen, around the door, and down the stairs. Cheers erupted in the basement.

Deb looked outside. Hail the size of marbles bounced on the lawn, but only a few drops of rain streaked the windows as yet. She saw a bolt of blue lightning reflected in the windshield of her car and hurried back to the basement.

"Now Dusty's behind the bubble machine," Cammy told her.

"I don't care where Dusty is," Deb exclaimed. She flopped into one of the lawn chairs and made a wild gesture toward the ceiling. "Let the whole house fall down. Quit screaming, Grub. I need to hear the radio."

But the transistor radio offered little more than scattered urgent words amidst blasts of static.

"How long do you stay down here?" Deb asked.

"Until the storm goes by," Eric said.

"Is the announcement on the radio?"

"Sometimes . . . or sometimes Dad tells us."

"Jesus, what a place," Deb sighed. "Middle of nowhere, and God's still trying to destroy it four days a week. Do you like living in Cypress?"

"We don't really live *in* Cypress," Eric said.

"Great. A pedant. I feel like I'm at work. You know what I mean."

"It's okay. I like living in a house better than in a trailer."

"Would you like neighbors? So that there were other children?"

He shrugged.

"Maybe you wouldn't get bored," Deb added.

"I don't get bored, usually," he said.

"I noticed you saved your baseball cards. Why not your astronomy project? Wouldn't you care if the storm wrecked all your hard work?"

Eric absently rubbed his itchy neck. "It's not hard."

"You could replace the baseball cards," Deb said.

"To replace this many baseball cards would cost a lot of money," he said. "We always have empty cans."

DEB HAD NEVER ACQUIRED *The Tonight Show* habit. If awake at 10:30 p.m. on a weeknight, she was working. Rather than try to compete with the monologue, she waited for the roar of applause that announced the first commercial break. When she heard it she plodded downstairs. Roy was on the couch, flipping through the Harper brochure. Because he heard me coming, she thought.

"Do not ever threaten someone I love again," she said.

"I tried to apologize," he murmured.

"I'm tired," Deb said, "so we can talk about Eric tomorrow."

"Take him."

She turned back to him. "Don't do it because you feel guilty."

"That isn't it," Roy replied.

"Then why?"

"Isn't it enough you win?"

"Eric wins," she said.

"Whatever you say."

When he made no appearance of going on she said, "It needs to be explained to him."

"You'll have to tell him about the school," Roy said, "because I don't know the details. But it won't hurt him to visit."

"He shouldn't be made to visit the place, Roy."

"You can't debate a kid his age. He'll go. All right?"

Deb stepped outside. The sky was clear. People had asked the stars to show the future since ancient times. Deb knew that no less a Modernist titan than Carl Jung held the predictive powers of the heavens in high regard. Had not the questions asked of the stars guided history? Where should I fight the battle? Does God approve of our new king? Reveal to me which tall dark stranger I will meet at the cocktail party.

Deb looked to them, too, but to her the stars' names were a mystery, the shapes they formed indistinct, their messages inscrutable.

THE TEAM MILLED AROUND waiting for Coach Garland, the more dedicated already paired up to play catch, the rest bent over to admire Eric's scabs and rashes. Tim Nevin pronounced the case beyond the allergic reaction his father suffered when he took penicillin. A collective *ooh* went up when Eric showed the impressive patches across his lower back and ribs. This was by far the most his teammates had ever paid attention to him. When they had done a full examination, excepting only those scabs covered by Eric's underwear, Nevin and Shraeder, the left fielder who only threw underhanded, argued over the relative miseries of poison ivy and poison oak, ranged then into bee stings and had just moved on to ticks when Coach Garland ordered the team to line up for the stolen-base drill.

Julie leaned close to Eric and held out a pinching pair of fingers. When he jerked back she glared at him. "I just want to pick the dead scab off."

"No," Eric exclaimed, and he hopped away from her.

"It won't hurt, it's just hanging there—"

Coach Garland shouted for Eric to get in line. When Eric explained, Coach added, "Julie, quit picking his scabs."

The team went through the stolen-base drill, Johnny running in from first, his brother Tim throwing from home plate, and everyone else lining up to take a turn tagging Johnny out. The first throw skipped by the entire row of players and into the outfield. Julie intercepted it, as instructed, and lobbed it back in to her father.

After a delay caused by several errant throws, Eric made it to the front of the line. He smacked his glove and took up a position astride second base. This time the younger Garland threw the ball right on target. As always Eric turned to take Johnny's charge, this time with his free hand—his meat hand, in Coach

Garland's language—stuffing the ball into the glove. Eric was so certain Johnny would try to slide around his perfect tag that he bent a little to intercept the lead foot. Instead Johnny slowed half a step to take aim and, turning a shoulder, crashed into Eric so hard that Eric flew backwards and tumbled over.

"Hey, he held on," Johnny said.

Eric struggled up, tears in his eyes. With the best throw of his career he struck Johnny square in the sternum. Johnny's face contorted into an expression halfway between shock and pain, and finally he doubled over. At the same time Julie charged forward, battering Johnny around the back and shoulders with her glove. Eric leapt into the fray, now screaming and crying. The rest of the team shouted encouragement to both sides. Coach Garland took Eric around the waist and tucked him under one arm, even as he tried to push Julie away. When she skipped around to Johnny's other side he called for Tim to take hold of her. A melee engulfed all the Garlands, most of the starting infield, and the center fielder.

When it was over, Eric was sent to the bleachers. Meanwhile Julie shouted names at her brother until Coach backed up his orders to desist with a single step in her direction. He then spent twenty minutes yelling at the team. When practice broke up, Coach Garland motioned Eric off the bleachers and met him at the third base line.

"You think you're in trouble?" he asked.

"Yes," Eric said, his voice cracking.

"Well, you're not. Johnny had it coming." The coach put a hand on Eric's shoulder. "Am I taking you home?"

The question surprised Eric. He had already accepted he'd be abandoned.

"Should I say I'm sorry?" he asked.

Coach Garland thought a moment. "I don't think so," he said in a low voice. "With Johnny, it's better if he's a little nervous."

ROY DIDN'T WASTE HIS ENERGY hoping for a raise. He wanted overtime. The rare person who bitched about working Saturdays saved it for his wife or friends, because his coworkers would kill him. Regular work paid the bills. Overtime paid for Christmas gifts and the unexpected trip to the emergency room. After a particularly good week it replaced a bald front tire.

Roy went straight from work to the tire store and stood at the counter waiting and taking in the odor of rubber. The opening chords to "Homeward Bound" made him perk up his ears. In his teens, God knew, he had sat in a few railroad stations, the ticket for his destination sharing space in a jacket pocket with a sandwich and candy bars and cigarettes and whatever pocket change was left. He bought the 45 of "Homeward Bound" after hearing it one time even though he lacked the money for records, and certainly for a record player. In those days before meeting Jean he spent ten months a year training and racing harness horses at tracks and fairgrounds from Madison to Memphis, from western Iowa to eastern Ohio. Sometimes he still felt his wrecks in one elbow, or on the odd occasion when something in his left shoulder sounded like a boot scraping gravel. Even the barn could be dangerous. He'd once lost his big toenail when a horse stepped on his foot. It had grown back as something that looked like gnarled, yellowed wood. When he listened to the song in those days he felt less nostalgia for home—where he knew he was unwanted—than the desire to have a home. The song's sentiments aside, Roy had been happy to hear intelligent lyrics on the radio. Rhyming "come back to me" with "mediocrity" had struck him as Gospel, and if now, ten years later, he believed no gospel of any kind anymore, at least the lyrics recalled that moment when he spilled out his thoughts on Simon and Garfunkel over the donuts and coffee that, unknown to Jean on her side of the booth, would serve as two, if not three, of his meals that day. They would sit there for hours. The song would play many times. His life would change. Soon to be alone no more. Soon to declare wherever she stood to be the center of the universe.

The next day, Gordon arrived at the site at quitting time. He was sweating through his second shirt of the day. As the crew began to leave he asked Roy to wait a minute, then spoke on the side with Tiny. Roy leaned against his car, trying to look nonchalant. He desperately wanted a cigarette, but he worried his hands were shaking too badly to light it. It frightened him that he did not know why they were shaking.

Gordon's tie streamed behind him as he approached. For a moment he turned a cheek to the flying dust. They traded greetings.

"I'm sure you've heard about this burglary," Gordon said.

Roy nodded.

"The police have to check all the leads. Including the contractors at the house—and that's Carl. Normally he'd be enough. But they want to talk to all of his coworkers. Just to dot the i's."

"Us," Roy croaked. He quickly cleared his throat. "Sorry."

"It's a formality. No one's accusing *you*. But if they talk to one guy they have to talk to everyone, or someone'll start bitching. Especially with these characters. I didn't want them to spring it on you. Jesus Christ, all your kids need is to see the cops at your house asking you about this bullshit, with everything else that's happened. But not a word to anyone else, Roy. I mean, not a word. Or it's both our asses."

"You told Tiny?"

"I had to, he's my best foreman. No point in offending him when I know he's innocent."

"You said they'll come to the house."

"Maybe it'll be here, maybe at home. I don't know. You can do this for me, Roy? Keep quiet?"

Again, Roy answered with a nod. Gordon patted him on the arm, mentioned his appreciation and the next day's work.

Roy drove home with a constant eye on the rearview mirror. A white car trailed him all the way to Cypress. As a test he turned into town, past the school. The white car continued down the highway. Once at home he asked Phyl to stay longer. He had an errand, and she had her doubts, but she agreed. Roy removed the bag of coins from the closet shelf, stuffed it in the pocket of his jacket. In the basement he dumped a battered metal toolbox onto a table, threw some old tools he no longer wanted back in, and then took it and his fishing pole.

Two cars had parked at the bridge. From the road he spotted familiar forms and shadows. To his relief no one had gone further than the edge of the trees. Once in the woods he followed the trail until he saw one of Eric's old bobbers swaying in the breeze. He put the toolbox on the rock shelf and threw out an unbaited hook for show.

First he placed the bag of coins onto the unwanted wrenches he'd left in the toolbox. Then he removed a spool of clothesline and pulled out what he guessed was twenty feet. After a look around, he tied the line's loose end around the toolbox's handle, knot after knot. When he was satisfied, he cut the clothesline and with many more knots secured the open end around the rusted tent stake sticking out of the ground.

At the water's edge he dipped the box into the water and let the weight of the tools drag it down. It sank into the muddy, bass-friendly depths with nothing more than a ripple.

Roy scattered sticks and dead leaves to cover the stake and the line. Here and there he placed larger chunks of wood on the line and pressed them into the soft mud. Finally, he planted a large rock half in and half out of the water to hide the few inches of line visible there.

On the way back to the car he felt his nose running. He paid it no mind until he wiped it and saw blood on his thumb. In the side mirror he saw a bright red stream curling around one side of his mouth. He stumbled into the house with blood all over his shirt. The girls screamed. Eric stared. Phyl hustled all of them aside and put down newspapers with a chair in the center. When Roy had soaked one towel she handed him another.

"Do you want the emergency room?" she asked.

"It'll stop," he said.

But it didn't. He got back from the hospital after midnight with a stopper bulging from the left side of his nose. The next day Roy met the sheriff's deputy looking like a boxer. A bad one.

Cowell arrived first in the blue Nova. He had, he said, called in a couple of favors with the sheriff to sit in on the interview. A rush of gratitude lit Roy's face.

Embarrassed by the reaction, Cowell gestured to his nose, said, "I heard you struck a gusher."

"The doctor who looked at me thinks it was hypertension," Roy replied. "At my age, for God's sake."

"They give you anything?"

"Pills to help me relax."

"Don't go taking one with an Old Milwaukee," Cowell said.

"Don't worry."

Roy had, however, taken one a half hour earlier.

"What's this going to be like?" he asked.

"Nothing to it. Tell him what you know, and that'll be that."

Deputy Daniels had a long head and sat straight up in his chair. Roy had expected to feel intimidated and, facing Daniels across the table, he did. Cowell sat to his left sipping coffee.

"We appreciate your cooperation," Daniels said. "Just a couple of questions, and we'll let you get to your supper." The deputy then asked how well Roy knew Dombey, if Dombey had said anything or acted strangely, if Roy saw him socially, whether he knew the owner of the house, how long Roy had worked at his present job, if anyone was to blame for his broken leg. As the questioning continued the topic returned always to Dombey.

"We've got a problem," Daniels said as he sat back. "Our problem. Not yours. Mr. Dombey isn't cooperating. Nothing says he has to, not yet, but it looks suspicious. You know he has a record?"

"Sure," Roy replied.

"When it comes to this type of crime, it's rare to run across a first-timer."

The statement hung in the air. Roy's first impulse was to speak up for Dombey. A couple of weeks earlier he would have done so, with all sincerity—Dombey had often expressed a new appreciation of freedom's little pleasures after his jail time. But Roy stopped himself. He had read enough crime novels to know that if Daniels had something on Carl, he would expect anyone in the know about the burglary to defend him.

"I'm sorry to hear that," Roy replied. "About Carl, I mean."

"He's not doing himself any favors," Daniels said. "You're sure he hasn't mentioned anything?"

"No."

"You knew he was working out there."

"He does a lot of work on the side," Roy said.

"Ever let you in on it?"

"He's asked once or twice. Not with this job, though."

"Why not?" Daniels said.

"I don't know."

"The broken leg," Cowell said.

"I forgot about that," Daniels said. "Busted my right one a few years ago breaking up trouble at the college. It's hard to miss that much work. You run up a lot of bills."

Sweat caused Roy to itch under his arms and between his legs. But the pill had steadied his nerves. And marriage had taught him to fake sincerity.

"You ain't a-kidding," he replied.

Daniels traded a look with Cowell, and Roy knew it was over. The deputy handed him a business card at the front door.

"If you hear anything," Daniels said, "and I mean anything, it'd help us out in a big way, Mr. Conlon. There's a reward, too. The whole system keeps you anonymous. If you have any questions, call me."

Outside the three of them traded thank-yous and good-nights. Roy turned to go inside. Cammy asked the inevitable question.

"Are you in trouble?" she said.

"No, no," Roy scoffed. "It's about a thing at work. Some tools were stolen."

"Not willingly."

Cowell said with wonder, "What's wrong with people?"

They were quiet, Cowell contemplating the many answers to his question, and Roy trying to decide whether to ask one of his own.

He finally said, "Dombey was about to talk to the sheriff, right?"

"How'd you know that?"

Cowell stared as Roy explained the conversation with Bramm.

"Ladd said they thought this Dombey was coming in with another guy," Cowell said.

"He and his brother-in-law were working on the house together," Roy said.

"Boy oh boy." Cowell leaned against the car. "I reckon they'll search their places. Was Dombey married?"

"He was in an old lady situation for a while but I think she left."

"Then I don't know how it works as far as getting permission, or if the sheriff needs any. Storm watchers don't get a lot of legal training." Cowell rubbed his jaw. Then a sudden thought changed his expression. "Hey, I know he was a friend of yours. I'm sorry and I should've said that first."

"It's a hell of a shock," Roy replied.

"How about we get something to drink inside?"

"You know, I think I'll sit here a minute."

When Roy finally followed him up the driveway he walked with straight and steady steps. He was sober, but not unburdened—as the shock wore off he realized he was suddenly, numbingly afraid. Grub stared up at him through the screen door. Roy leaned inside and picked her up, carried her onto the lawn. She babbled things he didn't hear.

THE APARTMENT DOOR WAS OPEN for the breeze, and a few of the party-goers greeted Fergus as he made his way through the throng. Once inside he edged into the mob and looked around.

"Hey, Mr. Spaceman!" A heavyset man in a fringed leather vest and battered jeans shambled through the crowd, his drink in the air, maniacal eyes spinning in opposite directions behind a pair of granny glasses. Centuries of graduate and post-graduate education were offended by his rough passing. He embraced Fergus with a bellow of laughter, and while the massive vodka-and-lemonade sloshed against the sides of his glass, it never spilled, not a drop, except what escaped his mouth when he tried to talk and drink at the same time. "The next step in human evolution," he said with a bow.

"Mr. Hill," Fergus replied.

The man held up both stubby index fingers, balanced the prodigious drink between the palms of his hands. "Rob Hill no longer exists. Today and from this day forward I am Captain Freedom Hill, come to transmit the revolution via guitar and drum. Drink?"

"Lead on," Fergus said.

Fergus said his hellos on the way to the bar. By the time he made it across the room Captain Freedom had mixed him a gin and tonic of Jovian proportions.

"That'll cure your malaria," Rob said, and he took two deep chugs of his drink. "See my piece in *Rolling Stone* yet?"

"I haven't had a chance to read it," Fergus said. "So what're the Eagles like?"

"Superb catering. Next week I start tagging along with Alice Cooper for *Creem*. Dumb music, but at least the guy's in on the joke."

"What's going on with this lady friend of yours?" Fergus asked. "Tommy said you had a new situation."

"Yeah. Last weekend in Buffalo I got two blow jobs, and then we had sex."

"Good for you."

"I hadn't slept in a woman's bed in a long time," Rob said. "I forgot how many pillows they have."

"As if that's supposed to make you more comfortable afterward."

The room continued to fill. Fergus spent a half hour politicking, sprinkling in some shoptalk, answering polite questions about Deb and the baby. Once his obligations were fulfilled he worked his way back to Rob. They returned together to the bar.

"You still writing the sci-fi?" Rob said.

"I'm trying to," Fergus said.

"Why'd you give up writing-as-art, man?"

Fergus shrugged, leaned against the wall between the door to the kitchen and the hostess's oak bookcase. "Because I'm not Norman Mailer or Saul Bellow. Why bother, otherwise?"

The familiar light of the drunken evangelist rose in Rob's eyes, kindled by prescription drugs and his natural fervor. "You have that Cheeveresque eye for little details," he said. "Have you considered my offer to write about music? Deny not the rock, brother. Ride an angel's wings via chartered jet."

"My wife is suspicious of me spending office hours with comely students," Fergus said. "What she's going to say when I tell her I watched a mother-daughter tag team plow through Grand Funk Railroad?"

"One man's debauchery is another man's anthropology."

"You possess great insight today, Grasshopper. What're you on?"

"Actually, I'm not sure," Rob said. "It was green, though. Greenish. I think it's intended for sheep."

"I have a question related to your career."

Rob froze in the pose of Rodin's *Thinker*.

"Do you have any idea how to reach Carole King?" Rob sputtered in protest and Fergus held up a hand. "It's for my eight-year-old nephew. He wants to send her a letter."

"He's how old?"

"You remember me telling you my sister-in-law died? This is

her son. I think he associates his mother with Carole King. That's my amateur psychologist bit."

Rob became thoughtful. "I associate my mother with an obese Eleanor Roosevelt."

"I associate your mother with Teddy Roosevelt."

"Yeah," Rob said. "The mustache, certainly."

"At first I thought he could send King a letter through her record company, but if she's ever going to see it, that isn't a realistic option."

"Waste of time," Rob said, nodding.

"I'm not asking you to hand deliver it," Fergus said.

"You're just trying to improve the odds," Rob said. "I'm with you."

"What do you think?" Fergus said.

For a moment the sound of a blender overwhelmed all voices. They used the opportunity to take great gulps of their drinks. A moment later the crowd around them cheered a newborn pitcher of daiquiris.

"Carole King, Carole King," Rob mused, snapping his fingers. "I can feel a synapse firing, but it's ... so ... far away. Let me search my memory banks—in a clearer state of mind, if you know what I'm saying—and see if I can connect someone to someone who knows someone."

"You're a real droog," Fergus said. "Don't sweat it if you strike out. Maybe we can catch her on tour."

"I doubt it, man. I think she has stage fright."

"I thought Carly Simon had stage fright."

"It's highly contagious," Rob said. "Every woman who comes near James Taylor gets it. Joni Mitchell's trying to head it off with an experimental vaccine."

AUNT DEB'S APARTMENT seemed cramped to Eric after the high ceilings and cross drafts of the farmhouse. Tall bookshelves crowded the living room, and the spines of the books and dark wood of the shelves drank up light. Shelves and dish racks crowded the small counter space of the kitchen; the hanging pots and pans and baskets of fruit seemed to lower the ceiling to an inch above Fergus's head. Files, stacks of loose paper, and library books covered every flat surface. The constant noise added to the closeness. At home he rarely heard machines, save the buzz of the clothes dryer when it finished or the ominous coughs of his father's cars. Here the racket of the elevated train shook the windows every eight minutes. The traffic was a constant hum punctuated with horns and yelling and the periodic approach and fade of the O'Jays via the Doppler effect.

Once Emma had dismissed him in favor of her friends, Eric went to the desk at the living room window. Fergus sat here to write. Eric halfheartedly explored the old black typewriter, its visible moving parts and the half-black, half-red ribbon. When he pressed a letter the key rose in salute. An adjustable desk lamp sat to one side; on the other a canvas sneaker held a stack of manila folders in place. He craned his neck to look up. It would be a clear night. How you could use a telescope with all these buildings around, Eric had no idea.

Probably his father would be grilling. If they had not come for him yet.

The sudden shock of worry made him close his eyes, the way he did before Johnny Garland plowed into him. Eric wanted more than anything to tell somebody. Not to find help for his dad. Just to feel better. To share the secret, shift it to someone else, someone else who knew what to do. It had to be someone in the family. It was that kind of secret, like Dad's drinking. But he couldn't go to Uncle Cowell or Aunt Phyl, since Cowell worked with the sheriff. Aunt Deb would never keep the secret—she'd be on the phone to Dad about it ten seconds later. On the way to the city he almost decided to tell Uncle Fergus. But probably it was a bad idea. Married people told each other things. It was just like Aunt Phyl and Uncle Cowell.

After dinner, they sat down to play Scrabble. Emma, required by decree to spend Sunday nights with her family, joined the game. When Eric pointed out the unfairness of playing against a writer, Fergus laughed.

"Do you ever play Scrabble at home?" Fergus asked as he arranged his letters.

"Some of the letters got lost," Eric said. "I play at the Garlands' sometimes."

They began the game in silence. Deb, sweating from the kitchen, shuffled around the table checking everyone's trays. Emma had segregated her consonants from her vowels. Eric had spelled ORION. When she came to Fergus, she saw he had spelled ZEBRA. As she passed he tossed the z into the box top and drew a new letter.

"Can't spell anything," he said. "Your turn, Em."

Emma looked up at Deb. "I've already spelled one word, and he hasn't scored yet."

"I have a feeling he will later," Deb said as she mussed Fergus's hair. Fergus raised his eyebrows.

The moment Eric put down ORION Emma raised a protest. To Eric's surprise proper names were illegal. Fergus tried to mediate an exception to the rule, but Emma, quoting the inside of the box top, appealed to her mother for a ruling.

"That is the rule," Deb said, "but Eric didn't know. Give him this word, but then he can't use proper nouns in the future."

As Eric scored only six points for it, Emma agreed.

"I thought you played before," she said.

"I did but the Garlands don't care about rules," Eric said.

The game was pleasant enough to make Eric think Emma might be willing to treat him like a cousin. When afterward he proposed playing cards, she claimed she had to do homework and slammed the door to her room. Eric knew Em was far too smart for summer school. He returned to the window and watched the shadows fall outside. Soon it would be the summer solstice, the longest day of the year. From that moment on the earth started its slow rise toward the upright stance of the equinoxes.

That kind of thinking had led to this mess, he thought. What was he doing auditioning for a school for smart kids? He didn't even understand force-outs at second. When he said this to Aunt Deb she replied that baseball was not important. In addition to missing the point—an ongoing problem with Aunt Deb, in Eric's view—her statement justified Eric's wish to attend school in Cypress rather than at Harper. If baseball was fun, that is, not a subject in a school, and if he still could not understand, let alone contemplate, why a third bunt counted as a strike but a third foul did not, if that "blew his mind," then what chance did he have with the Declaration of Independence or musical notation or the themes of long paragraphs? How smart would he need to be to figure out the theory of relativity? The math aside—and Eric held out hope that so-called advanced mathematics still lay on the other side of fractions—there was the everything-happens-at-once-at-the-speed-of-light idea. At times, thinking it over late at night, Eric thought the concept just out of his reach. It was good that astronomers worked at night, then, because during the day he had absolutely no idea what it meant.

He had a feeling he would need to be Einstein to succeed at Harper, and with Aunt Deb he made it clear he fell somewhere short of All-Time Genius. According to Fergus, however, Einstein had so much trouble speaking as a child that his teachers considered him hopeless. The story made Eric think. He respected the strange mental powers of people like Ed Arndt, a kid who had trouble writing his own name, yet was able to identify any hood ornament in the world. Still, he doubted Ed Arndt or Cammy or any of their classmates would grow up to propose important scientific theories. More than anything Einstein and Galileo and other geniuses thought in a unique way. Books made it clear that unique thoughts were an essential part of genius. Did a genius, then, possess unique words to express the unique thoughts that set them apart from others? Did the lack of such words explain why Eric could not make his father or Julie or his aunts or uncles understand him, or what he did, or what he wanted?

Roy once came into his room, saw him sitting cross-legged amidst the constellations, and shouted, "Is that all you ever do?" The frustration and anger were obvious.

What else was there to do? Cassiopeia had to be finished.

The contradiction confused him. All these people expected him to learn. *Pushed* him. At the same time his attempts got him yelled at, or threatened with a new school, or charged with know-it-allism. A year earlier, before the constellations, he'd tried to combine learning with making money. He invented a board game inspired by a class project on the states. During his research on his assigned state—North Carolina—Eric studied a map that showed the state's various resources. A picture of a tiny leaf represented tobacco, a picture of a tiny lump of coal represented coal mining, and so on. In his game, he assigned dollar values to each of these resources. Players, in some way he never worked out, accumulated new resources for their state or country, swapped, say, minerals like coal or gold for food like wheat or pumpkins. Whoever made the most money won the game. Eric believed it would become as famous as Monopoly and make him and his family millionaires. Cowell approved, as he did of all get-rich schemes. "Don't forget me on your big payday," he had said. His father told him to go out and play. Eric did not remember his mother's reaction at the time, only that she brought it up while fighting about money with his father, something along the lines of, "Now Eric thinks he has to work." It was not necessary to crouch at the heat vents to hear her. During those fights you could catch every word from the garden. Eric soon abandoned the game.

Fergus came into the living room with an armload of sheets, blankets, and pillows. As he made up a bed on the couch, he saw Eric maintaining a stare out the window.

"You shouldn't worry about tomorrow," he said.

"Yes, I should," Eric replied.

"It'll be easy. What constellation are you going to talk about?" Eric sighed as theatrically as possible. "Scorpio, the Scorpion. It has one of the brightest stars." He turned in the chair. "Did you ever have to go to a special school?"

"Man, I'm not as smart as you."

"You're lying," Eric said, facing away again. "You're a professor."

"Not yet," Fergus said. "Don't jinx me."

"Aunt Deb says Mom would want me to go to Harper."

Fergus paused to tuck the sheet beneath the cushions. "When did she say that?"

"In the car once."

"Regardless of what your mom might want," Fergus said, "you should go to Harper for yourself."

"Because Mom's not coming back."

"That isn't what I mean." Fergus moved the blankets and pillows aside, sat on the end of the couch. "I'm not going to tell you she's coming back. A part of me is religious, but I don't pretend to understand the ways of God. I'll leave that to Aunt Phyllis, you dig? Just keep one thing in mind, Eric. When we pass away we don't just vanish. We're made of energy. Energy cannot die. It cannot be destroyed. That's one of the firmest rules in science. None of us, nothing, is gone forever."

Eric was obviously confused.

"Do you know how the universe began?" Fergus asked.

"The Big Bang," Eric said.

"Right. For billions of years after the Big Bang, but long before the Earth formed, atoms linked together to create new forms called elements. Atoms are tiny bits of matter. They make up everything—the gases in the Crab Nebula, the feathers in this pillow, your dog, the plants in your garden. Everything. In the universe's early days, these atoms came together and formed new stars and all the other phenomena out in space. After a while some of these atoms linked together to form planets. The atoms changed shape—maybe from gas to rock or liquid—but they never disappeared. Billions of years passed. Life forms appeared on Earth. Bacteria, worms, clams—"

"Trilobites," Eric said.

Fergus snapped his fingers. "Trilobites. Exactly. Seas full of them. It's like this, Eric. All the life forms needed to consume energy to live—the way you eat food to live. They took in the energy in their food, whatever it might be, and changed it into energy to make their bodies run. And then other animals, needing energy, ate *them*, to make their own bodies run. Atoms in dead animal or plant bodies changed into tissue in new animal bodies, or the atoms became coal or oil, or turned into nutrients in the dirt that were used by other animals and plants. That's just a few of the many ways energy changes form. You're made of atoms, Eric. Billions of years ago the atoms that make up you were a part of stars. Then those atoms were parts of animals—maybe trilobites, maybe dinosaurs, maybe saber-toothed cats. Some of your atoms have been in plants. They've been rocks and minerals. They've been water and ice. Little bits of you, these atoms, existed in countless other creatures and in countless other forms."

Fergus reached over and turned the chair so that Eric faced him.

"Then, eight years ago, they all gathered together and became you. Some of those atoms came from your dad and some came from your mom, and then some from these other sources. So, see, she can't really die." Fergus put a hand on his shoulder. "It's true the person you knew is gone."

"She's gone," Eric whispered, and he nodded.

"But she's going to be a part of a billion other things," Fergus said. "She's going to be starlight. She's going to be flowers and rain and the spaceships taking human beings to new planets. She's going to be everything. Forever and ever, until the universe ends."

Eric stared ahead, trying to understand. "Is that true?" he finally asked.

"It's the law."

The bedroom door creaked open down the hall.

"Speaking of the law," Fergus added in a low voice.

Eric tried to speak, to tell him about the coins. But Deb inter-rupted. After her cleaning regimen—not only bathing and clip-ping nails but flossing and putting balm on his remaining patches of red skin—he returned to the couch for encouragement and a good-night kiss. The voices down the hall rose a moment, then fell. He waited for sleep, missing the murmur of his radio, and finally, just before he dropped off, studying the billions of years on his fingertips in the glow of the yellow streetlights.

THE INTERVIEW TOOK PLACE in one of Harper's science classrooms. There were two rows of high black tables, each with a sink in the middle and three stools behind it. A Periodic Table of the Elements chart covered much of the back wall. The windows looked out onto the roof of a movie theater. Deb, at Maria Spinoza's nod, took a seat at one of the lab tables. To her dismay the wind had blown Eric's hair in all directions. And somewhere between the front door and the room he'd developed an untied shoelace.

The interviewers sat in ugly plastic chairs brought from the teacher's lounge. Maria was in the middle. On her right reclined an elderly man with white hair like cotton candy. The buttons around his middle threatened to fly off. All he needed to be an Oxford don, Deb thought, was a pipe and thicker ear hair, though the mustard-colored slacks might make up for those shortcomings. To Maria's left sat a stunning black woman with the regal head and face of West African sculpture. Deb had no doubt the woman's sweeping, multicolored robe had been purchased firsthand from the weaver.

Eric waved when introduced. Does he think he's driving a tractor? Deb thought. Maria gestured to Dr. Wallace, the old don, and to Dr. Gill.

"Eric," Maria began, "your aunt has told us a lot about you already. What we want to do is ask you questions about yourself. It's not a test. We're merely curious. Do you understand?"

Eric nodded.

"Try to answer out loud," Maria said.

"I understand," Eric said.

At their request he ran through the roster of his family and the matter-of-fact news that his mother had died. When he finished, Dr. Gill asked him about his house. Eric paused, surprised. What could you say? A list of appliances ran through his mind, but Dr.

Gill leaned forward and spoke again.

"What I'm asking," she said in her deep voice, "is for you to provide a little detail on what it's like to live where you live. You mustn't have neighbors close by, is that correct?"

"Not too close," Eric said.

"And do you like where you live?"

Eric wanted to answer yes—an answer enough for him and anyone in Cypress—but Aunt Deb had insisted he always say more than yes or no.

"I like having my own room," he said. "It's a drafty house in the winter, though. Sometimes. My dad tries to save the heating oil so he doesn't always turn on the heat. We use oil in a big tank. When the truck comes Dad and the truck driver have a smoke while it's pumping. They complain about the Arabs."

Deb tried not to put her head in her hands.

Now Dr. Gill leaned forward with intensity. "And they don't like Arabs? What do you think of Arabs?"

Eric, sensing conflict, returned to his upright posture. His heart had started beating harder.

"I don't know about them," he said, "except they have camels and oil. And—" He cut himself off.

"And?" Dr. Gill said.

Looking at the floor, Eric murmured, "And a long time ago, they named a lot of the stars."

Unable to help herself, Deb said in a low voice, "Explain how you get your water, Eric."

"You pump it yourself?" Dr. Gill said.

"Yes, because we have egg water."

"Egg water?" Dr. Gill said.

A look from Maria kept Deb from leaping in again. She wanted to scream. How often had she used the word *sulfur* in the last twenty-four hours? In the cab ride over she had told him to say the water had a sulfur smell. Even as Eric paused, no doubt intimidated by Dr. Gill, Deb closed her eyes, called on her understocked reserves of calm. The way it was going, about three more questions would induce labor.

"Every few days my dad goes to the park and pumps good water," Eric said warily, "or he goes to my Aunt Phyl's house."

Dr. Gill desisted, a half smile on her face. Maria moved on. She
asked Eric to explain what he considered fun. Eric rattled off a
list: his telescope, playing cards, TV, the garden, Julie Garland. As
he spoke he began to fidget, felt the tie clinging to his throat, the
black socks suffocating his feet. Aunt Deb had mentioned nothing of these kinds of questions. What did it matter to teachers?

"Don't you play baseball?" Maria said.

Lectures from his father on Coach Garland's generosity made
Eric reluctant to admit how much he hated baseball. If a .000 batting average and near-constant terror was the price for Coach's
rides in the pickup and the company of his daughter, Eric felt
obliged to pay, but that was the only reason he did it. Mumbled
answers and shyness got him nowhere, though; Maria continued
to ask questions.

"I'm the worst player on the team," he finally said. He waited in
vain for his aunt to contradict him.

"The worst?" Maria said.

"Even Julie is better, and she's not really on the team."

"Why doesn't she play?" Dr. Gill said.

"Because she's a girl," Eric replied. Dr. Gill frowned. At the
same moment Deb felt the baby kick. The shock set her ribs to
vibrating. She closed her eyes. When she opened them she knew
all three of the interviewers had caught her grimace.

"Do you think that's fair?" Maria said. "Would you care if she
played?"

"No."

"Even if it meant taking your place part of the time?"

That was as close as Eric came to laughing. "Julie wouldn't play
right field," he exclaimed. "The worst player plays there, like me
and Ed Arndt. Even the second graders on our team don't play
right field, so Julie wouldn't. She can catch grounders and line
drives. She'd play a good position like third base."

Dr. Wallace made a great growling noise in his throat, the
kind of noise Aunt Phyl made before spitting. "If I may ask a

related question," he began. He sounded to Deb like a laryngitic Katherine Hepburn. "Mr. Conlon, am I to understand you play the outfield?"

This new interrogator startled Eric into silence. He answered with a nod, then hastily added, "Uh-huh."

"Let me ask, when you throw a ball back to the infield, do you throw it straight?"

"Almost never," Eric said, relieved at the easy question. "Mostly it goes sideways. Sometimes backwards."

Dr. Wallace cleared his throat again. "How do you *intend* to throw it?" He held up one hand palm down, brought it in a line across his chest. "Straight?"

This sounded like a test to Eric. He strained to remember Coach Garland's instructions on long throws.

"If it's a long throw," Eric said thoughtfully, "we're supposed to throw it like this." Mimicking Dr. Wallace, he drew his hand across his body to show the arc of a proper throw. "On a lob. It goes further."

"Why?"

"The ball goes further up, and goes a longer ways forward before it comes down."

"Why does it come down at all?" Dr. Wallace asked.

"Gravity," Eric said.

The old man's face lit up. "Ah, you know about gravity?"

"Only a little," Eric said. At that moment he noticed the untied shoe. Even as he spoke it hammered away at his attention, and he fought the urge to bend over and tie it. "In my books," he stammered, "it says scientists study gravity with math. That's bad luck for me. Math's my worst subject, except for penmanship."

For a moment Dr. Wallace paused in thought, hands folded across his stomach. The other interviewers half turned to him. Deb recognized the strategy, something she had been too anxious to do when her own daughter faced the same questioning. Maria focused on personality and personal expression. Gill handled background, both socioeconomic and moral, though no doubt for her the two were intertwined. Wallace, the retired mathematician, had charge of science.

The old man gestured. "Why don't you show us the contents of your box? We hear you have devoted a great deal of energy to the project."

To Eric's relief the points of light showed up well on the low ceiling. He briefly explained the plain facts about Scorpio, the Scorpion, that it was best seen in summer, that Antares, the red star at its heart, was a first-magnitude red giant. The Arabs came up again, too, since they named it. He then explained how he made each constellation.

"Tell us," Dr. Wallace said, "are the distances between the stars to scale?"

Scale? Eric thought. Did scorpions have scales? Like a dragon? That was Draco.

"I don't know what that means," he answered.

Silence filled the room. Eric wished to be in orbit around Antares, 250 light-years from Harper Elementary School.

"I copy the constellations out of a book," he stammered.

"Do you measure the distance between the stars in the picture?" Dr. Wallace asked. "Say, with a ruler?"

"With a tape measure," Eric said.

"Don't you own a ruler?" Maria said.

"The tape measure is better. It bends." Tears welled up in his eyes. He felt his heart pounding. "My dad," he said, trying to gulp down the tears, "tried to show me how you can measure and then multiply. To make something come out bigger, so it's not dis . . . dis . . ."

"Distorted," Deb said softly.

A chuckle came from Dr. Wallace's beard.

"That's just what we're talking about," Maria said.

Eric said nothing.

"Do go on," Dr. Wallace said.

"It's hard to figure out because there's decimals," Eric said, distracted by but afraid to wipe the tears on his cheeks. "At my school, you don't learn decimals until fourth grade."

There was murmuring between the adults. Eric thought he might be free, but Dr. Gill again leaned forward.

"You said that your father tried to teach you, correct?" she asked. "What does he do for a living?"

"He builds houses for this guy, Gordon," Eric said.

"He's a carpenter," Deb added.

That seemed to satisfy some unasked question. Maria glanced to either side, to see if her companions were finished, and then addressed Eric once more.

"At Harper," she said, "we like to encourage the students to work with their hands, the way you did with your project. But, obviously, a lot of learning comes from books. Students here have to read a lot, Eric. Much more than you do at your current school. When you went to Akhmatova, I bet you were encouraged to choose books and read on your own."

"We could go to the library anytime," Eric said.

Dr. Gill crossed her legs. "What was the last book you read?"

"That I finished?"

"Unless you're reading one now," Dr. Gill said.

"A non-astronomy book, if you please," Dr. Wallace added.

Eric thought a moment, back to returning his library books on the last day of the school year. "*Chariots of the Gods,*" he said.

"What was it about?" Maria asked.

"The cover said it was about flying saucers, but I didn't understand very much of it because of the big words. My dad had to tell me what they meant. Except he said that book was mostly, um, it's kind of a bad word. But I did read the little part next to the pictures. By myself. About how the aliens on the flying saucers painted gigantic pictures in the desert so that their spaceships could land, and how there's flying saucers in the Bible."

Deb wanted to but did not cover her eyes with a hand. As subtly as she could she turned her face from the interviewers, to hide her emotions, and heard Wallace say in his shaky voice that Eric sounded like quite an enthusiast.

The interview ended with handshakes. Maria escorted them through some of the downstairs classrooms and labs, as well as the library, before saying good-bye at the front door. Once outside Deb and Eric turned onto a busy street and crossed to the other side despite honking and sirens. Deb did not look at him or say a word. At a second crosswalk they paused to wait for the light. He thought she might speak then, but she kept her eyes straight ahead, as if trying to move the signal with the power of her mind, like the guy on TV who bent spoons. A block ahead, she pointed to a neon sign overhanging the sidewalk. It read *Deli*.

"Fergus is waiting for us," she said.

"Are you mad?" Eric said.

She knelt down and put a hand on his shoulder, her expression unreadable behind her sunglasses. "I'm not mad in the least, honey. I hope it's a long time before you have to endure an ordeal like that again." She paused, as if to add something, and suddenly motioned ahead with a jerk of her head. "Let's get lunch for you."

As they entered the restaurant Eric gazed at the baskets of bread lying out, at the salamis hanging from the ceiling. Fergus sat at the front counter drinking coffee and reading the newspaper. They caught his attention, and he slid off the stool.

"I'll bet you're starved," Fergus said to Eric.

Eric pointed to the daily specials on the chalkboard behind the counter. "What's lox?"

"Smoked salmon."

"Is it good?" Eric asked.

"It tastes like the inside of an ashtray," Fergus said. He loosened the knot of Eric's necktie. "Let's get you out of the clothes of oppression. How'd they treat you?"

Eric let out his breath, the sigh of ball four and waking from bad dreams into sunlight.

THE NEXT MORNING DAWNED hot, still, and sticky. Deb lounged naked on the edge of the bed while Fergus dressed for his trip to the zoo with Eric. When he finished he came to the edge of the bed and leered at her breasts.

"A dramatic difference, isn't it?" she said.

"They're spectacular. Can we keep them?"

He kissed each and returned to the piles of papers stacked beneath the windows. Each stack was held in place by books, ashtrays, or—in one case—a candle that dripped wax in seven different colors.

"Wasn't I reading the apocalyptic plague thing in bed last night?" he asked.

"You put it in your case so you wouldn't forget to take it to the office," she said. "Try to get Eric back here by four. If I don't beat the worst of the traffic it'll be midnight before I get to Cypress."

"The heat should wear him out pretty fast," Fergus said.

"I don't look forward to going."

"If you want my advice, wait until you hear he's in before you sit down with Roy. That way if they say no there's no unnecessary hard feelings."

"Eric will get in," Deb said.

Fergus, distracted by combing his hair, spoke offhandedly. "If he does, try to convince Roy instead of steamrolling him. When you want something, you get relentless. I imagine two little men in uniform inside you twisting keys simultaneously."

Deb turned to face him. "Once Maria calls," she said, "Roy needs to make a decision right away. As the person doing the work on his behalf—no thanks to him, by the way—I think I deserve to have my voice heard."

Pink had already risen in her cheeks and on her chest. Practice had taught Fergus that Deb liked best to argue when she felt she had the advantage. That might mean pressures of time or superiority of argument or, as was usually the case, intensity of emotion. Once she started a fracas she never backed down. The only benefit for him was that such times were when he had her fullest attention and received the fullest hearing.

"The adversarial process won't work," he said quietly. "Roy knows this is an excellent opportunity. But putting aside the fact Roy's lost his wife and faces the prospect of losing his oldest child—"

"Then let him do a better job," she said.

"Deb," he exclaimed. "You don't go to a man and tell him he can't raise his kids. You've been married twice. You have brothers. Surely you understand something about the male gender."

"Oh, so that's what it's about," Deb said.

"Roy has to make the decision. What's so wrong with letting him make it and keep his pride, too?"

"Macho bullshit," she scoffed.

"He knows he's barely making it," Fergus said. "Maybe he gets through the day by blaming the hard times on Jean's death. Not without some justification, by the way. Even he knows that excuse won't work much longer, though. You like to correct men on their unenlightened attitudes, Deb, but you're the one judging Roy by old criteria. I mean, what's the traditional image? He's supposed to move on. Duty above all, don't succumb to grief, don't make mistakes."

"He was an alcoholic before Jean died," Deb said furiously.

"So what?" he replied. "Jean was an alcoholic, too."

The moment he said it he was sorry—more for picking a more intense fight than for saying something she knew, as well as he did, to be a bald truth. Yet for a moment Fergus wondered if she did know. Did the gauze of loss so alter the image of her sister? He knew Deb was wise. Surely she saw, as he did during their visits, the three or four beers per night, every night, the casual dispatch of the kids to the refrigerator, Jean's unpredictable rages, the vague disdain when Fergus switched to iced tea after one beer, or when Deb—who preferred wine to beer—abstained altogether.

Surely she knew, as he did, the stories of Jean lounging around in her underwear, no doubt too pleasantly buzzed to question this decision. Surely Deb did not take Eric, the source of the stories, as imaginative enough to dream up bizarre Oedipal fantasies?

"I can't believe you'd say that," Deb gasped. "Jean did everything for those kids. If it wasn't for her Cammy wouldn't know how to read, she wouldn't be able to hold a spoon. She'd be in a home, where the doctors wanted to put her in the first place."

"I'm not saying Jean lacked virtues," Fergus said. "Just that she had vices. They lived the way they do now when she was around, so as far as the socioeconomic picture goes, not a thing has changed. Look, I'm not trying to dishonor the dead. But Roy would never say the truth to you, not even in his own defense. I know he's got problems—"

"Oh, can you admit that?"

"It doesn't make him unfit to raise your sister's children."

"You're wrong about all of this," she said. "But I guess men always stick together."

Now his voice rose. "How can we do otherwise, in the face of such unmitigated virtue? The woman threw a pan through a window, Deb, and she damn near brained her kid doing it. I once watched her insult her own son because of the way he dressed himself. He's six years old, and she made fun of him, and you know why? Because she was impatient and hung over all the time and held the same grudges and had the same mean streak as you." He stopped himself. Now he did mean to dishonor the dead. "Forget it," he said. "I'm leaving the field. I didn't know her well. I do know Roy a little. Deal a blow to his pride, Deb, and you'll lose Eric."

"Maybe Phyllis should remind him that pride is a sin," Deb said.

"So is wrath," Fergus said. "You should keep that in mind."

DEB TRIED TO TIME HER ARRIVAL to miss Phyllis. Instead she found Phyl and Cowell snapping green beans at the kitchen table with Roy. A pyramid of corn gleamed nearby. Deb gave an abbreviated report of the interview. While she praised Eric more than she reported on the school, Phyl's expression did not soften. Deb called in Fergus and they left, twenty minutes after arriving.

Over dinner the others quizzed Eric on his opinion of the school and the city—Phyl had particular worries about the dangers of the latter. As they rested from the feast Eric passed with his telescope over his shoulder like a rifle.

"I'm surprised you left that at home," Cowell said.

"Uncle Fergus told me it'd be hard to see stars in the city," Eric said on his way out the door.

"All those tall buildings?"

"And too much light."

"Then why's he need to go?" Phyl muttered.

"Hush, Phyllis Lynn," Cowell said.

"I just don't like it that he'd be separated from his people."

"It isn't that far away," Roy said.

With a disapproving murmur Phyllis rose to clear the plates. "I'm not talking about the distance," she said. "I think people ought to stay with their own. The Bible states the family is the foundation."

"Here comes the chapter and verse," Roy said.

"That's all I'm going to say."

Cowell said, "If you don't behave we won't let you go to the fireworks later."

"I'm not coming anyway," she replied. "Too much noise and too many mosquitoes. The fireworks won't be any different than they were last year."

Roy and Cowell went onto the porch. The long, pink, diminishing trails of airplanes hatched the sky, each line seemingly bound for the same vanishing point beyond the horizon. The swing creaked as Cowell rocked. Roy, standing on the bottom porch step, watched Eric screw the telescope to its tripod and set it up on the trunk of the Ford.

"This damn humidity's killing me," Roy said.

"I heard a meteorologist interviewed on the radio," Cowell replied. "He said a dense pocket of humid air had hung over the center of the United States since early spring. That's why there've been so many tornadoes. Been a hell of a summer all around. You must have a hard time up on those roofs."

"I definitely wouldn't turn down a million bucks to quit my job," Roy said. "You want a smoke?"

"Not with my physician so close," Cowell said, and he thumbed toward the clatter of Phyl clearing the dishes. "You shouldn't mind Phyl. What's she going to say? Eric's like her own. All the more so since Jean died. You know Phyllis. Everything is crystal clear now that she's found Jesus. Personally, I think my Holy Trinity's a lot easier to understand—Ford, Chrysler, and GM. I've got Detroit, and she's got Jerusalem. She doesn't see it that way, though."

"I doubt he'll even get in," Roy replied. "There's no use fighting about it."

"Even if he does, this isn't a deal where Eric falls through a trapdoor if you make a bad choice. Either way has its points. That's a good situation to be in, when you think about it."

The image of Libra passed through Roy's mind. To various ancient peoples the constellation formed an Altar, a Lamp, or a Chariot, and then Claws, and eventually the Scales. "Weighing, weighing," Eric had chanted, moving his outstretched hands up and down with the shifting of imaginary weights. Roy, remembering that moment, laughed to himself.

"What?" Cowell said.

"Nothing," Roy said, and then he laughed again. "I swear to God, I don't know where the damn kid gets this stuff. He's even got me thinking about it."

Toward dusk they packed into Roy's Ford and departed for the fairgrounds. In honor of the fireworks Eric had read up on the Chinese invention of gunpowder. It came under a section on rockets. On the left page: two jaundiced men in ponytails standing next to a tube that emitted a sparkler-like explosion drawn to look like brightly colored asterisks. Toward the end of the section, a photo of a Saturn V booster lifted off from the bottom of the page. Once Roy, Cowell, and the kids were on the road Eric leaned over the front seat and began sharing this knowledge. By the time they reached the fairgrounds Cowell had convinced Eric the Chinese had landed on the Moon five hundred years earlier.

Cowell also mentioned his plan to abandon the flea market. Eric had worked with him that morning, gasping in the heat and humidity while Cowell went around checking the radiators of old ladies. This gave Eric the chance to be a salesman. He ended up getting rid of a bunch of old license plates. When Cowell returned to the table Eric held up a pair of dollar bills.

"One for you," Eric had said, "and one for me."

"How do you figure?" Cowell had replied.

"You said I got a share."

"You get a commission," Cowell said with mock outrage. "That doesn't mean half the sale. You can keep it this time, though. Hey, maybe you want to try to double your money on a game of Go Fish."

Eric had stuffed the bill in his pocket. "No, I don't."

"Couple of hours in that school, and you're smarter already."

Eric preferred the idea of fireworks to the actual show. Twenty minutes of it and he wanted to explore the food booths below. Cammy cried into Roy's shoulder next to him—she hated loud noises, yet always insisted on attending fireworks and air shows and parades led by howling fire enginery. Grub, sitting on Eric's lap, appeared alternately awed and bewildered. She finally fell asleep during the cannonade finale, twitching at each boom.

Eric volunteered to carry Grub back to the car. No easy job— she was growing faster than he was. As they walked Eric hurried up alongside Cowell. "What are you reading?" he asked.

Cowell slapped the magazine in his back pocket. "Almost forgot," he said. "It's an article on buying gold. Next year I'm letting the machinery of wealth do the work."

"You have enough money to buy gold?" Eric said, impressed. "Does he, Dad?"

"Any day now," Roy laughed.

"Don't you listen to old boy here," Cowell said. "The trick is, you buy gold at a cheap price, then sell it at a higher price, then wait and use that money to buy more of it cheap, then sell high again. A little luck, and you get richer and richer."

"Why do you want to be rich?" Eric said.

"Damn," Cowell exclaimed. As soon as he said it, he slowly looked around for offended parents. "There's not much else worth being," he said in a lower voice. "The song says there's two kinds of people—'Cadillac buyers and old five and dimers.' And I'd like to be the other thing once in my life."

As they pulled out of the parking lot Roy turned on the radio. Eric looked out the window, listening to a man sing that a waitress wouldn't light herself on fire for him anymore. The song had the qualities he associated with music on the college station—meandering melody, a quiet mood, and lots of lyrics he did not understand. He asked Roy to change the station, to no effect. That meant a long ride. Commercial breaks were the best reason to turn the dial, but breaks were very rare on the college station.

When they dropped Cowell off, Eric took his place in the front seat. "How long will it take Uncle Cowell to get rich?" he asked as they left town.

"I don't know," Roy said as he tapped his cigarette out the window. "I can't see the future."

"You could at the speed of light," Eric said.

"Oh, yeah?"

"When you go at the speed of light, time does this thing where everything that's happened, and everything that's going to happen—in the future, I mean—it all happens at once. So even though you're living right now, you can step into any time you've ever lived or will live in the future. Something like that."

The vanishing dashes of the highway center lulled Roy into trying to grasp such a thing.

"Did Fergus say how you're supposed to get up to light speed?" Roy asked. "Are we supposed to climb into a UFO?"

"I read in my book that sometimes a UFO crashes and the Air Force hides the spaceship in a top secret place."

"Don't go believing shit like that. I've got enough crazy relatives."

"You're good at fixing cars," Eric said. "Maybe you could repair the UFO."

"If you find one, let me know."

Lightning bugs smashed against the windshield. Eric imagined them as stars and himself as the passenger in a spaceship.

"Is it true, about the speed of light?" he said.

"Fergus knows more about science than I do," Roy said.

If the speed of light did open the future, perhaps it opened the past, and his mother filled the past. Could that be true? Eric looked up at Roy.

Feeling the stare, Roy feigned interest out the window and waited for the question he guessed to be on Eric's mind. Perhaps Fergus had even suggested the possibility. Roy found it a comforting thought, too. Could you pick and choose your moments at the speed of light? Unaware of the smile on his face he turned, and Eric smiled in return.

Did he ever think about Jean? What did he think, and why did he not say so? Did he feel, too, that to speak would open wounds as wide as the past? Each asked these questions of the other, Roy in conversation with himself, Eric from a deeper place that did not admit language, one receding even now, to be longed for anew in the distant future, when wisdom had proved to him the inadequacy of words, yet cheated him of the secret of saying the right ones.

ON SATURDAY, THE SIXTH, the Earth reached aphelion, just over 94.5 million miles from the sun. Fergus was reading a note about it in Monday morning's paper when the phone rang.

"Good morning, Asimov!" said the caller.

"Rob?" Fergus said, raising his voice to be heard. "You sound like you're on the Moon."

"The dark side of it, man," Rob exclaimed. "Los Angeles. I haven't slept since Denver. Listen. No dice on Carole King. Confirm the new album in a couple of months, but negative on the contact information. When I get to New York I can—"

A commotion interrupted him. Fergus strained to hear. There were grunts and swearing, a loud bang as the phone hit a wall or floor.

After a long pause the voice of an ax murderer or roadie came on the line. "Is this Shaky?" he screamed.

Fergus hung up. The phone rang again an instant later. He picked it up with a tentative, "Hello?"

"It's me," Deb said. "I'm through with Maria. They're offering him a half scholarship. I'm leaving for Cypress right now."

WHEN ROY GOT HOME from work he saw Eric in the garden. Grub staggered nearby amidst the hung linen, swatting at it until it knocked her down then struggling to her feet to try again. Roy scooped her up for a kiss and called a hello to Eric. Eric waved without looking up and bent to examine the first green tomatoes on their vines.

Deb sat at the kitchen table, working the crossword in one of the Chicago papers. Despite having two fans on her she looked sweaty and miserable. Roy thought back to Jean carrying Grub. Just two summers ago.

"I made lemonade," Deb murmured.

He nodded.

"They accepted him, Roy."

"That was fast," he said.

"It didn't seem that way to me."

"I haven't been able to really think about it," Roy said.

"There isn't much time." She spoke softly, but Roy felt her intense stare as he poured lemonade. "By now you must be leaning one way or the other. If the school doesn't hear from us by the end of the week, Eric's spot will go to another child. We're only getting this long to decide because I'm connected." Deb paused to allow an answer, but Roy remained quiet. "You said he liked Akhmatova," she continued. "Jean was happy with his progress there."

"The money," Roy said.

"Half of it will be paid for."

"I thought those scholarships were for poor kids."

"You pump your own drinking water. You're poor." Deb took a deep breath. A few words in and she already missed Fergus's moderating influence. "What would Jean have wanted?"

"Doesn't matter. We can't ask her and there's no way of knowing. Look, Eric's happy here. The girls want him here."

"He'll be around," Deb said, her voice rising. "Most weekends, during breaks, and over the summer. Emma's situation with David is very similar, except you'd get Eric the entire summer. People do this, Roy."

He lit another cigarette, flung the spent match at the ashtray. It missed. A tiny black halo opened on the wicker place mat beneath its head.

"You know," he said sharply, "Cammy needs a special school, too."

Deb reached and lifted the spent match off the wicker. "Let me give birth to my child," she said, "and then I'll start taking care of yours. Never mind that my work may be a waste of time—"

"I didn't ask you to do anything," Roy said. "You're just taking control again."

"You would have never started. You never start. Anything. You survive, Roy. You endlessly survive. Nothing else. You're a give-a-shit about yourself and you're teaching the same thing to your kids."

Deb stopped herself. Somewhere in the back of her mind Fergus told her to retreat, but his voice was far away, behind many doors angrily slammed shut.

Roy mistook the pause for an opening. "You don't know what you're talking about," he said.

She slammed her hands against the table. The ashtray, the wicker place mat, Roy—all jumped in unison. "It should've been you," she exclaimed. "Somehow you survive everything. Every lapse in judgment. Every ugly little incident. Do you think if the positions were reversed Jean would not find a way? Do you really think that?"

"She made her choices," Roy said.

"She didn't choose," Deb cried. "Choice didn't lead to her out to this barn you live in. It was because this was the best you could do, and she loved you and she couldn't stand the thought of hurting you by asking for what she deserved. Jean was passing you by, Roy. Why do you think she quit so close to the end? Every day she sat in her classes absorbed in things totally unconnected to you. That life meant something to her, while at the same time it had less and less to do with you."

He motioned to the room. "I guess this life didn't mean anything."

"She couldn't have both and she couldn't admit to herself that she regretted the decisions she'd made. She made a choice, all right. To maintain. To put her strength and passion into enduring misfortune instead of avoiding it. Don't you dare say another word, unless it's to give thanks she made the choices she did, because nothing in her love for you had to do with the future. She always went with her feelings in the here and now, and she felt passionately about you."

"Some people would find that admirable," Roy said, but without much strength.

"I don't. I'd rather have her alive."

"It's not my fault she isn't," Roy said. "And it's not my fault she didn't take care of herself. She was afraid to face being sick. You don't think she suspected long before she got sick?"

Deb gave a derisive laugh. "Why would she deny reality, Roy?"

"Like I said, she was afraid to face it."

"That's insane."

"Sometimes I think so, too."

"She wasn't afraid of anything."

Roy shook his head. "She told me herself she ignored the signs. The lump they found—shit, she knew about it a year earlier. She found it herself."

"You're lying," Deb said.

"If I am, then she was lying. The same thing happened to her mother and she couldn't face that it was happening to her when she wasn't even thirty years old. That's the truth. So whatever you want to think of me, Deb, think it. I don't give a shit. But I'm still here, and Jean isn't because of what she chose on her own."

"I'm not listening to this," Deb said.

"Yeah, well, Jean hated to be disagreed with, too."

Deb unplugged the fan, jerked it out of the window. It crashed onto the floor. "Decide in the next twenty-four hours, Roy. I'm going upstairs to lie down."

ROY SAT STARING AHEAD for he did not know how long. Slowly the sounds of the world returned. An airplane passing over. Crickets chirping from the dark under the porch. At some point Cammy stormed in and asked if the fighting was over. Instead of answering, Roy sent her off to watch TV, which was her reason for asking, anyway. Looking down, he noticed ashes clumped on his jeans. He rubbed them into the fabric with his thumb.

Outside sweeping white clouds reached up over the western horizon like two immense hands. Eric stopped bouncing a ball against the garage. Roy noticed Eric glancing at him over his shoulder. In one panicked moment, Roy spotted Grub asleep in her car seat. Eric had opened the windows and, following a piece of advice from Cowell, spread a blanket across the windshield to block the sun.

"Why is your sister sleeping in the car in this heat?" Roy asked.

"Aunt Deb was screaming," Eric said. The ball hit the ground, bounced against the garage door, and popped into the air before coming down into his glove—*thump, bang, smack*. But when at rest his shoulders slumped. Roy thought that if a kid could look like an old man, Eric did.

"That's Aunt Deb," Roy replied.

"What about?"

"Telling me my faults," Roy said.

Thump, bang, smack.

"Do I have to go to Harper?" Eric said.

"That's still up in the air."

"It's not fair I can't choose."

"Yeah," Roy said. "If you're lucky we'll let you pick who you marry."

Thump, bang, smack.

"I heard you say Mom's name when you were arguing," Eric said.

"It mostly concerned your mother."

"Would she really want me to go?"

"Hard to say, son."

"At light speed I could ask her," Eric said.

"We'd all have a few questions. I better go get Grub."

Roy reached into the car and scooped up Grub. He was on the way back to the house when Eric said, "Wait." Roy did, but Eric had trouble saying whatever came next.

"What?" Roy finally asked.

"I don't want you to get mad," Eric said.

During the last part of the exchange Eric came closer. But he stopped out of arm's reach. Roy thought the child had shrunk even more; it looked as if his bones and nothing else held up his clothes. Though his chin was down Roy could see the blood in his face. Pity filled Roy, and in an instant he wondered why, and then realized he saw himself in Eric, maybe for the first time.

"I won't," Roy answered.

It was a struggle, but Eric said, "I heard you talking to the policeman." He studied Roy for a reaction. There was none.

"I didn't mean to," Eric added in a frantic whisper.

"Okay."

"You said it was about tools. That's what you *said*."

The reproach in his expression quelled whatever anger Roy might have allowed around his promise. Eric had first looked at him that way at six months. Roy remembered the day. It was the first time he'd seen his child bleed. He had gotten too close to the skin while trimming Eric's thumbnail. Nothing serious. Eric had cried, though not for long, and he had looked exactly as he did now.

"I know I did, son," he replied.

"Did you steal them?" Eric said.

"No, I didn't."

"But I heard."

"Carl, the guy I worked with, took the coins. He asked me to hold on to them. I didn't know they were stolen. When I found out I made him take them back." Eric breathed hard, wiped his eyes. "When he got in the wreck, that was the end of it. I can't really tell you any more."

"Why?" Eric asked.

"I just can't."

Eric glanced back at the house, lowered his voice again. "Did you tell the police? When you were outside?"

It took all Roy's control to not answer right away. He wanted to say no. He was tired of lying. But no led to why not, and to what happens if they find out, to him asking Eric once more to never tell, and to truthfully answering his son's inevitable question about what would happen if he did. Roy did not need to weigh his fear of the consequences against the guilt of burdening Eric with that secret. The moment he understood his choices he bent down, the better to see into Eric's face.

"Yes," he said.

IT WAS BEFORE 8 A.M., and only one other car was parked on the bridge. As Roy handed the poles to Cowell, an old-timer with a gut trudged up the path and told them nothing was biting.

Cowell turned. "Fish have to bite on the first day of vacation, right?"

"It's only right," Roy replied.

"I can't stay too long—I have to drive up to Rockford to get parts for the Nova."

"That's fine."

The heat had already settled in. Cowell wiped his face three times during the walk. For some reason Roy hurried ahead. By the time Cowell arrived at the new can't-miss fishing spot, Roy had put down the coffee thermos and tackle box and opened the bait container.

"This humidity's bad," Cowell said.

"Like walking through water," Roy replied. "Chicken livers okay?"

"I'd rather fish with them than eat them."

Cowell lit one of Roy's cigarettes, concentrated on the smoke and the excuses he might use to explain the smell on his clothes. Roy handed over the first rod, then went to work on the second. A few cars rumbled over the bridge—people on their way to work. Around them the birdsong fell off as the sun climbed and the day's heat began to set in. Roy pitched his line out underhand toward the middle of the river. For a while they waited in silence. So long, in fact, that Roy worried he would run out of time to say what he wanted to say.

"Did you hear any more on the burglary?" he asked. "Did they close the case?"

Cowell wiped his forehead with his shirtsleeve. "They can't because Dombey could've really been coming in to give them information. But their main goal now is finding out what happened to the loot. No coins turned up in the car except good old American spare change. Same at his trailer. Next week, the sheriff's taking down the billboard about the anonymous tip line and putting up a new one about a reward for the coins. It sounds like that's about all he can do."

"What a waste," Roy said. "The whole thing."

"That it was. I was just thinking about it last night. Those coins—damn, Roy, how much could you sell them for? Not enough to even take off from work for a few weeks. He'd have paid up his bills, fixed one or two things, maybe, and then he'd have needed money again."

Roy let out a little more line. "That's a tough place to be," he said.

"I can't imagine things ever being that bad," Cowell said.

"Can't you?"

A chill crawled out from a place deep inside Cowell. "What I mean is," he said, "is that I don't understand why he'd have taken that kind of change for nothing more than a little breathing room."

Roy didn't seem to hear him. "Sometimes you get so caught up in things, you lose perspective."

"Easy money."

"That's right."

Licking his lips, Cowell said, "I'm as guilty as the next guy about that. But it isn't ever easy for most of us."

"That's the funny thing," Roy said. "It's only easy for people who already have enough."

"Maybe we should head back," Cowell said. "Nothing's going to bite in this heat."

"There's something—"

"Listen—"

But Roy spoke louder. "To your left. Off the rock. There's an old tent stake, right next to where I put the thermos."

After a moment's hesitation Cowell put down the fishing rod and stepped off the shelf. The clothesline remained tied around the stake—a tangle of knots. He turned to Roy, but Roy was staring at the water. It took an effort, but Cowell lifted the line through the mud and leaves and sticks. He followed it to the water's edge. With the toe of his boot he freed the line from under a flat gray rock, tugged to feel the weight, and suddenly dropped it as if it had become electrified.

"The whole collection," Roy said. "I sank it with a few wrenches inside that old toolbox from the trunk."

"Son of a bitch," Cowell breathed. "All this time?"

"I got spooked keeping the stuff at the house."

Cowell ran one hand then the other through his hair. "I guess I know the *why*," he said, "so the how doesn't matter. But—Lord, Roy, all you had to do was ask."

"I couldn't ask again."

"They'll never stop looking. Not those boys. To them it's the crime of the century."

"I'm tired of worrying about it, Cowell. Tired, period. If you want to drag it up I'll help you."

A thousand cover stories passed through Cowell's mind, and thoughts of the reward money, and a vision of his picture in the paper. But he was shaking his head before he got that far. Hurriedly, a little clumsily, he wrapped the clothesline around his right hand, took hold of it with his left, and began to pull. Roy joined him. Cowell freed his right hand and asked Roy to pull. Needing a better angle, Cowell inched into the water, felt for the drop off with his foot while pulling hand over hand. The box came up without any trouble. Cowell told Roy to take the weight and, reaching out as far as he dared, he took the wet end of the clothesline an inch above where Roy had tied it to the box. With his right hand he fumbled a switchblade from his jeans, opened it, and sawed through the line. The splash caught them both. In a moment the toolbox had disappeared. Cowell watched it sink as he thumbed the frayed end of the line. When he had caught his breath a little he let Roy pull him back onto the bank.

Roy put the meat of his hand over one eye and against his cheek, felt sweat there. Was it sweat? "Boy," Cowell sighed, "this is a hell of a day."

"I'm sorry for bringing you into it," Roy said. "For bringing anyone into it. I was going to lift it up and drop it somewhere but I was afraid they'd find my fingerprints on it."

Cowell rolled up the line and cut the other end free. The tent stake he wriggled loose and tossed into the woods. By then shock had worn off and he felt tired.

"I'm sorry," Roy said again.

"You haven't done me any harm," Cowell said, with a hand on Roy's shoulder. Roy began to shake under his grip. Cowell did him the dignity of staring at the water and of not speaking again until the shoulder had become still again. "Nothing in that box is worth what would come next if you owned up. Not even to that rich old judge, though maybe he'd think otherwise."

Roy let out a heavy, damp breath. Cowell patted his arm, sighed.

"Don't think about it," he said. "Not about the money and not about your part in it. All guilt's going to do is drag you down."

"You think I should tell them?" Roy said.

"We'd both be in trouble now."

"What a fuck up."

"It's a pretty good one," Cowell said, and he tried to laugh. "You must've been overdue. I'll tell you what. Get the poles, and I'll put the tackle box back together. Better give me another of them cigarettes, too."

Cowell absently chose a different way back to town. Too late he realized the road threaded past Dombey's trailer park. Yellow police tape still cordoned off the mobile home. Behind it was a weedy piece of field gouged with tire tracks from kids mudding on their minibikes. Cowell noticed a man with a metal detector sweeping the ground around a clump of scraggly coneflowers. It had been a hard morning, but at least Roy had saved him twenty years of doing the same thing.

DEB MANAGED TO GET Eric to submit to a haircut, and after a lot of wrestling bought new shoes for both of the girls. When the kids had been sated by ice-cream cones, Deb bought herself a second root beer float for the road, much to the delight of Eric and Cammy, who cheered as she put it away on the way to Phyl's house.

As she pulled into Phyl's driveway she regretted making a doctor's appointment for Grub. Deb wanted a nap more than anything, would have gladly stretched out in the backseat. Phyl came onto the porch wiping her hands with a dishrag. She ordered Eric and Cammy inside and, to spare Deb getting out, stood at the side of car.

"Roy's been by," Phyl said.

"Why isn't he at work?" Deb said.

"He showed up about ten. Sober, but telling me stories. There was a sack in the backseat of his car."

Deb had to admit that Roy's willingness to face Phyl showed a lot of guts.

"To hell with him," Deb said, and then she winced at cursing in Phyl's presence. "If it's okay, Phyllis, let's just stick with our plan. I can't cancel a doctor's appointment because Roy's playing hooky."

"It looked like he was headed toward the house. Doing his drinking there ought to be safe enough."

Deb returned to Phyl's for Eric and Cammy almost two hours later. Neither of the children seemed to have any idea of what probably awaited at home, and Deb admired Phyl's self-control. Rather than ruin their mood, Deb said nothing on the way. They knew something was wrong the moment they saw his car at home, regardless. From the dining room Deb heard tools and movement and music overhead. She had hoped he would be passed out by now, and she considered driving away again.

Her worst words from the night before came back to her. With beers in him he might be up to anything. How many times had he tossed everything Jean owned into the yard? She said nothing when Eric fell into step behind her. Each creak of the steps should have warned Roy, but whatever he was doing, it created more than enough noise to mask their approach. The work was going on in Eric's room, at the far end of the upstairs hall. A half-dozen beer cans lay scattered in the doorway. The hammering ceased. Deb first caught sight of Roy's shadow. She went in, her hand on Eric's shoulder, and said Roy's name.

He looked down from atop a stepladder. Twenty-five cans of various sizes dangled from fishing line strung back and forth across the ceiling. He was in the process of stapling up strings of white Christmas lights. At intervals the pine green wire disappeared inside each hanging can and then reappeared on the other side to run to the next can. Roy had unscrewed most of the bulbs, not all but most, and dozens of the discards were scattered on the bedspread.

"Get down from there," Deb said.

"Let there be lights," Roy exclaimed. "I wanted to get those big bulbs—you know the ones—they're like that big, big as your thumb."

The stepladder turned beneath him and with a loud whoop he tumbled to one side, leaving the string of lights dangling from the ceiling. The bed frame snapped spectacularly when he landed. Deb cried out, but Eric turned away and only heard the thump as Roy's head cracked against the headboard. Before either could move Roy got to one elbow, grinning dumbly. He gestured to the ceiling and with the broken bed's help got his unsteady legs under him.

"Not such a bad father," he muttered, still smiling. "I can finish later." He took a beer can from the dresser, shook it, tossed the empty onto the floor. "There's another one for you," he said to Eric. "Maybe it'd be good for one of the smaller ones."

Deb stepped aside to let him stagger out. But Roy halted at the door.

"Now wasssh this," he said, flipping the switch.The constellations lit up from one corner of the room to the other. Eric realized that Roy had taped bulbs inside each can. Above Eric hung

Orion, banged out from the bottom of a can of apricot juice, the white light showing through the large holes for first-magnitude Rigel and Betelgeuse, and for those that marked the famous belt, and the smaller holes of the other stars. To Orion's left were Taurus and Hercules and Cygnus, and behind it Scorpio and Ursa Minor, and to the right, in a long line stretching down the length of the room, Eric saw Virgo and the botched attempt at Draco, Boötes, and Cassiopeia, Canis Major, and Perseus, half finished.

Roy's footsteps receded, and the door slammed shut down the hall. Deb absently kicked a few of Roy's empties as she wandered around the room. The green wires, she noticed, were bare. Roy had unscrewed all of the bulbs not inside the cans in order to simulate a night sky.

Eric turned to her. "I never thought of this idea," he said.

The breeze from the window had caused Cygnus to turn and Deb stopped the can with her fingertip. After a moment Eric flipped off the light switch.

"Aunt Deb?" he said.

"Pick up these empty beer cans," she murmured. "Then come downstairs. Let him sleep."

THE BAG OF CANS landed with a crash in the center of the garbage pit. With a gesture Roy pointed Eric to an old railroad tie and they sat down side by side. Eric folded up into himself, hands tucked between his knees, elbows close against his body, ankles crossed.

"When I was fifteen," Roy said, "I left home. It was scary. Part of me didn't want to go. I'd never been on my own like that and I had to leave my younger sister—your aunt Pam—behind. You know why I went?"

"Why?" Eric whispered.

"Because it was a chance to do better than I was going to do at home," Roy said. "What happened to me, son—you see, my parents weren't so good. They didn't do things for me that parents should do for their kids. It's hard to explain, but one of the most important things a parent can do is get his kids ready for the world. Because when a person grows up and leaves home, it's like starting a long trip, and your parents, see, they have to provide you with what you need to make it through the trip—to make it through life. Do you understand?"

Eric nodded.

"My parents didn't provide me with much of anything," Roy said. "Not even love, really. So when I left there was this road ahead of me, and sometimes it was hot, the way blacktop is in the summertime, and sometimes it was wet, or icy and dangerous. And they sent me out to walk it without any shoes."

Roy put his hand on Eric's back as he felt him begin to cry.

"If they had," he continued, "things would've been easier for all of us. For your mother, too. I'd have been taught things instead of having to learn as I go. I remember a few weeks ago, you had a baseball on the dining room table, and you were moving it to block another ball. You remember that? It's good to learn things on your own like that, but you need people to show you the way, too. Believe me, there's a difference. Sending you to this new school, son, it'll give you a head start, it'll expose you to people who'll teach you things and provide you with some of what you need. You won't get hung out to dry."

"What if I don't want to be an astronomer?" Eric declared.

"There are a lot of other things to do," Roy said. "This'll give you the best chance to find one that makes you happy. To find out what you ought to do."

"I have to go to the school," Eric whispered.

"Yeah, you do."

Eric closed his eyes as gravity pulled him into a new orbit.

THE BUILDINGS AND CHURCH STEEPLES were black against the last blue-green light of day. Venus glimmered far above. Eric inched forward on the platform to see it.

"Not so close to the edge!" Emma yelled, pulling him back. "Stay out of the blue area."

Eric instead studied those around him. An old, large black woman stood tapping her foot to the tune she hummed. A balding young man dressed in hospital scrubs paged quickly through a much-abused *Sun-Times*. Near him a young woman with long, brown hair chewed at her gum, and when she caught Eric looking she gave him a smile. As Eric turned back to Emma he noticed a stern-looking man dressed in black, thoughtfully strolling down the platform, the night breeze whipping at the helixes of hair dropping from beneath a wide-brimmed hat. The longer they waited, the more people arrived, young men talking and tired cleaning ladies rolling their eyes and waving their arms as they complained in Polish about their workdays.

The train's headlights came into view. With much clattering it whipped onto the track alongside the platform. Eric flinched and stepped back, even as the others crowded forward to where they guessed the doors would stop. Exasperated, Emma called for him above the noise and smacked her thigh to underline the urgency.

Crowding in with the rest, he took special pleasure in stepping into the blue area. Emma took a seat next to the man in scrubs. Rather than stray in search of a place to sit, Eric took hold of the bar near her seat with both hands and, as always, stumbled when the train pulled from the platform. Through the doors he watched Venus as it followed them north.

At home he accepted a kiss atop the head from Deb and explained his day as fast as he could. Fergus's typewriter clattered behind the bedroom door.

"Do you have homework?" Deb said.

"I have to rehearse my presentation."

"That's all?"

"And Spanish," Eric added. "Spanish at school isn't helping me. On the train I can't understand people when they're talking in it."

"They're just talking fast," Deb said, not looking up from cutting onions. "Go rehearse."

"Will you listen?" Eric asked.

"Later. Go practice on Aidan."

Aidan sat in his mechanical swing looking confused. After turning off the swing Eric gently brought the seat to a stop. Aidan looked just as confused. Eric dragged over a foot rest, arranged his presentation on the floor, and after a pause to clear his throat picked up a sheet of paper.

"Presenting a report on northern constellations by Eric Conlon," he said. "I think you will like this part, Aidan. The Big Dipper is also called Ursa Major. It is one of the most recognized constellations. In other parts of the world, people have thought the shape looked like a chariot, a bull, or a wild boar. In France, instead of the Big Dipper, it is called the Big Saucepan."

He placed his flashlight in the can's open end and turned it on. Ursa Major appeared on the fireplace cover.

"All of its stars are of the third magnitude or brighter, making the Big Dipper very easy to see. It's a circumpolar constellation. This means it's seen every night of the year in the Northern Hemisphere. It's never seen in the Southern Hemisphere because it turns around Polaris, the North Star."

Eric now returned to addressing Aidan. "Ursa Major means *Great Bear*," he said. "It moves around the Pole Star that's in the tail of the Little Bear. The Little Bear, Ursa Minor, can be found by using the stars at the end of the Big Saucepan and going up twenty-eight and three-quarters degrees. My father told me once that the Big Bear circles the Little Bear to protect him."

#   #   #